The Billionaire's BET

ROSE M. COOPER

OSHUN
PUBLICATIONS
oshunpublications.com

Also by Rose M. Cooper

Can't Buy a Billionaire Series

A Virgin for the Bachelor Billionaire

Training the Billionaire

One Night with the Billionaire

The Billionaire's Bet

The Billionaire and the Biker Chick

The Billionaire's Billboard Proposal

Bobsledding with the Billionaire

Snowed In With the Billionaire

Accidentally Married to Her Billionaire Boss

Bought by the Billionaire

Bargaining with the Billionaire

Persuaded by the Billionaire

Unmasking the Billionaire

Romancing the Billionaire

AVAILABLE
IN AUDIO!

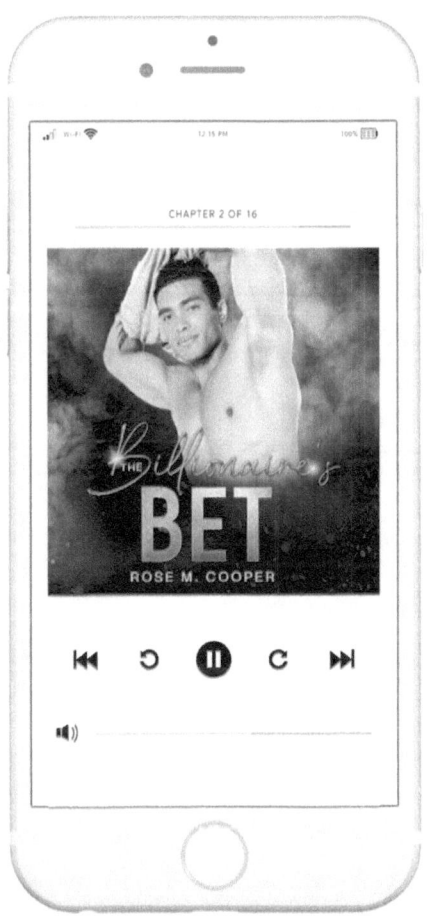

CHAPTER 2 OF 16

THE Billionaire's
BET
ROSE M. COOPER

GET YOUR GENRE FIX
TODAY! JOIN MY
NEWSLETTER FOR MY
RECOMMENDATIONS AND
UPDATES!

ROSEMAECOOPER.COM

CHAPTER 1
Time to Slow Down

KASE CHAPMAN WAS A DASHING, handsome young man. He owned several reputable multi-casinos throughout the States. At age thirty-two, he had already acquired eight different casinos and resorts across different states in the US. He was known as the casino owner and had the best turn-around in the industry.

Most of his peers held him in high regard for his no-nonsense approach to business and his commitment to a professional work ethic, but he didn't look like a billionaire.

When Kase was informed of what was happening right under his nose at the Silver Palms Salt Lake Casino, he felt as though someone had thrown him in the ring for a ten-round bout with Mike Tyson—with no prior training or warning.

He was known to be hard on his staff when it came to discipline and sticking to the rules when it came to gambling codes. He'd worked relentlessly for the last decade, pouring his blood, sweat, and tears into building each of his resorts. Whenever he acquired a new location, he made it his top priority to ensure things ran smoothly. This was his business method.

He'd just been thrown a curveball of epic proportions. He discovered that Austin Craig, head of operations at his Silver Palms Salt Lake Casino, had been discreetly embezzling funds. Nobody knew how long this had been going on. It was flagged during a random audit that Kase used to order for each of his casinos whenever he felt like it. It was his way of keeping everyone on their toes.

The massive casino was bustling with its bright lights and slot machines, spitting out coins intermittently. It was packed, as usual. In the back office, not even the walls of the supposed sound-proofed conference room could contain the rage in Kase's voice as he was firing off one question after another.

"I need you to tell me exactly how long this has been going on, Austin, and what sort of figures am I looking at here?" he shouted. "Has this been a one-off incident, or have you been skimming off the top for a while? Dammit, you need to answer me, or you're going to find yourself facing all the various authorities on this one." It looked as though one of the veins in his temples was about to burst. It was pulsating so rapidly.

Austin had been managing operations in Salt Lake for a little over five years. This was the first time Kase had been informed of embezzlement in the casino. His casino! Kase had been monitoring the numbers for Salt Lake for a while now. It had been all over the place, rather than functioning like the well-oiled machines of his other casinos. Could this be the reason why? He was pleased he had the foresight to go with his gut instinct in ordering that the random audit be done. He was totally devastated by the results of the audit. It's never pleasant to hear that you're being betrayed by someone you implicitly trusted.

This wasn't Kase's first rodeo, and he'd had to deal with

theft before, especially while the resorts were in the transition phase between being acquired. He personally trained key personnel on how he wanted things to run. He never had to deal with any of his general managers stealing from him, though, and it hurt like hell.

"Austin, I trusted you with running everything operationally, and I am feeling totally betrayed at this point. All that I need to know is whether there were any other staff members involved, and give me a number—even if it's an approximate one." He was beginning to calm down but remained frustrated by the tight-lipped nature of someone he'd considered a loyal employee and friend.

The silence in the conference room became deafening, and Kase eventually hammered the final nail into Austin's coffin.

"You've left me no choice other than to get the Salt Lake Police Department involved, the FBI, and the Gaming Commission. You know they'll have your license for this, and you'll never work in another casino again. I'm really sorry it had to come to this." The only response Kase received was a very solemn grimace as Austin stared down at the plush burgundy and gold carpeting that ran throughout the casino.

The silence was broken by Kase's phone's ringtone. The caller ID showed "VICKY".

"Oh shit, here we go again! I'm going to have to bail on this woman for the second time in just as many weeks."

"Hey, Vicky, yeah... I'm sorry to have to do this to you again, but I'm still in Salt Lake at the moment and have no clue what time I'll be back in Vegas, or even if I will make it back to Vegas this evening." Kase and Vicky had only been on two dates before this. Although the youthful, charming croupier from Silver Sands Vegas was interested in pursuing a serious relationship with Kase, the feelings definitely weren't mutual.

It was something Kase knew he would never be able to

commit to. His heart belonged to a girl back home, someone who had hurt him badly but nonetheless was indeed the only love of his life. Anaya.

Just the thought of her made him feel a bulge. Hopefully, nobody else is paying too much attention.

"Why, Mr. Chapman, I do think that this is the second time you've stood me up! You may just have to do something special to make it up to me." Vicky's voice was sensual, and she spoke with definite sexual overtones.

When Kase arrived back in Vegas, he'd have to explain to Vicky that things between them just weren't going to happen.

Right now, he needed to focus entirely and finish with the Salt Lake matter so he could try and tie up all the loose ends. Being responsible for more than fifty thousand permanent employees across the eight casinos was challenging. It was days like today that he wondered whether it wouldn't just be worthwhile to cash in his stakes in all the casinos and choose a quieter lifestyle somewhere. Days like this made him sick to his stomach.

He thought of retreating to his vacation home in San Diego. He'd bought it for himself on his thirtieth birthday but never got the chance to use it. What was the point of having it if he was never going to use it?

When it came to Kase's dating profile, you might say he was a bit of a player. Who wouldn't want to be seen next to the gorgeous six-foot hunk of a man? Managing multiple casinos was a daunting task. Hell, just being able to manage one of them successfully could prove challenging. However, Kase had quickly risen through the ranks of the gaming industry, taking one calculated risk after another. Fortunately for him, most of them paid off handsomely.

After a decade in the business, he became a legend within the gaming industry. However, while he was always flawlessly groomed and ready for any curveball that could be thrown at him on any of the floors of his casinos, he found this massive adrenaline rush to be his passion. It was what helped him get up in the morning and face each new day with anticipation.

There was only one ingredient missing for his life to be absolutely perfect—the girl who got away. The one who stole his heart. He had always imagined that they would be doing all of this together. While the industry thought he was a bit of a playboy, the truth was that he only dated as many women as he could as a means of trying to forget about his true love.

Boarding the Gulfstream 650ER homeward bound for Vegas, Kase poured himself a stiff double KWV on the rocks. It was sheer indulgence to drink one of the hotel's most expensive imported brandies, but what the hell? After a day like today, he needed something to take the edge off.

Running two major casinos right next to each other on the Vegas strip kept him extremely busy. Being the only resorts adjacent to each other, it made sense for him to convert one of the penthouse suites at the Silver Palms Vegas Hotel into his permanent living quarters. Vegas was like home for Kase. His reason for never getting around to San Diego was that, in a decade, Kase had hardly taken any time off. The word "vacation" was missing from his vocabulary. The only time he got out to San Diego was when he was visiting the casino nearby.

Sipping on the dark amber liquid, Kase caught himself thinking of Anaya again.

He chastised himself for thinking of her to the point where it was torturous. "She's probably married with a couple of kids running around. A beautiful girl like that isn't going to stick around waiting for me to sweep her off her feet. Besides, she broke up with me. I'm an asshole for even thinking about her," Kase would usually lament.

Pouring himself another brandy on the rocks, he settled in for the rest of the flight to Vegas, exhausted. He was pleased he'd called off his date with Vicky. He was well aware that she was after more than what he could offer her. His only reason for dating so many different women was that he didn't have to commit to any of them. No matter how many there were, none of them held a candle to the love of his life.

Arriving in Vegas, his car was already waiting for him. However, it wasn't an extremely long drive to the Silver Palms in Vegas. Vegas at night still made his heart beat faster, seeing all the lights, the people, and experiencing all the sounds from each of the casinos. This was the very lifeblood that he'd dreamed of most of his life. The only thing missing from this picture-perfect life now would have been Anaya, the woman he had so much love for.

Kase took his private elevator up to his suite and was completely overcome with fatigue. Usually, he would do the rounds at the different tables, stop in and greet all the staff, and possibly even have a drink in one of the theaters. For some reason, the events of the day had left him physically and mentally depleted. Unable to keep his eyes open, he didn't even bother getting undressed when he entered his room. After managing to take off his shoes and unbutton his shirt, he was fast asleep within minutes of his head hitting the pillow.

At 5:00 a.m., Kase was up and ready to hit the private gym. His personal trainer, Daniel, was waiting for him. Daniel noticed that Kase wasn't looking like his usual upbeat self.

"You okay today, Kase? You don't look like you're with us this morning yet," Daniel asked.

"I'm wonderful," Kase lied. The truth was that he could feel his heart pounding in his chest a lot faster than it should be at a resting position.

After warming up, he headed to the treadmill to start his cardio workout. Then he moved on to the stepper machine with the intent to push himself even harder than he did on the treadmill. It felt like he had slight indigestion. He chalked this up to not eating correctly and ignored the pain. Beginning his reps on the stepper, alternating with skipping, he'd no sooner started with his second set of skipping reps when the entire room suddenly went dark and everything around him felt surreal.

Fortunately, Daniel was within arms' reach. He stopped Kase from taking what could have been a nasty nosedive into some heavy gym equipment. Out cold, it took Daniel a few minutes to revive Kase. In the meantime, the receptionist made an emergency call to Dr. Ethan Stone, the primary on-site medical doctor for the Silver Palms Vegas and Silver Sands Vegas.

"I'm fine, really, Daniel. There's no need to fuss over anything. I was lightheaded because I didn't have dinner last night or breakfast this morning." Kase insisted there was nothing to worry about. He asked for some water and tried to stand up. Daniel insisted that he remain exactly where he was until after Dr. Stone had examined him.

"Daniel, I'm perfectly capable of walking myself to Ethan's consulting room and actually seeing him there. I'd like to hop in the shower before then, in any event." Kase usually sounded a lot more assertive and sure of himself, which made Daniel even more concerned about the overall health of the hotelier. After several unsuccessful attempts to get up on his own, Kase eventually agreed to remain where he was until Dr. Stone managed to see him. Sure enough, 15 minutes later, Ethan Stone walked in.

Taking one look at Kase, Dr. Stone would have been able to give him a reasonable diagnosis without even examining him properly. He had never seen Kase looking completely drained. There were only a few people who had watched Kase rise through the hospitality and gaming ranks as quickly as he had, and Ethan Stone was one of them.

Personally, Kase hated doctors because they reminded him of home. He was pleased that Ethan had arranged to examine him personally instead of sending one of his junior interns.

"Thanks, Ethan. What's up, Doc? Indigestion or heartburn?" Kase managed to joke, as he could now sit up with assistance. His head was still spinning, and the pounding in his chest had subsided slightly. But each of the symptoms was still there.

Nobody could fault Kase for his level of fitness. For his age, his six-foot frame was muscular and well-defined. He had to be if he was going to be successful and on top of his game in the hotel industry. He needed to be ready at the drop of a hat to be called to any of the casinos he owned.

The look on his face said it all. Clearly, Kase wasn't expecting the answer he received from Dr. Stone. One of his oldest and dearest friends was advising him to take a month's vacation where he could get away from anything and everything casino-related. Warning Kase that his situation was serious, Dr. Stone said he needed to unplug from all communications for at least a month.

"For a month? You have got to be kidding me. Do you realize that part of the time I'm going to be away is right at the beginning of the summer holidays? You know how crazy things get around here. Wouldn't it be better to wait until after the summer break when things quieted down substantially?"

"Kase, I don't think you quite understand how dangerous this is. I'm actually afraid for you right now! If you value your life, you will take what I'm telling you seriously. The next time you collapse, you may not have people around to help you. You're actually playing with your life right now. I know you think I'm just some fuddy-duddy out-of-touch doctor, but you know I don't mince my words, so here's the straight-up, no-bullshit version for you! If you don't go and get some rest, you spend a long time recovering. Your ticker isn't sounding good right now, and if you're telling me that you started with these chest pains before you walked in here this morning—well, you're just lucky you happened to be right here."

The longer Dr. Stone talked, the more ominous the diagnosis. Although Kase had initially recoiled at the idea, he was beginning to identify the uneasiness in Ethan's voice as well as the concern all over his face.

Where would he go? He only had his penthouse suite at the hotel as well as his holiday home in San Diego. By the sounds of things, he needed to be around a support system that wasn't going to add to his stress levels. San Diego was out; there were just too many staff there with prying eyes and there was no way he wanted any of them playing nursemaid to him.

There was only one other remote place where he would be able to get peace and quiet, which was his hometown. Just the thought of returning to his childhood home was enough to elevate his blood pressure even further. Was it the thought of returning home after so long, or was it because of Anaya?

What do you even pack for a month away in the middle of nowhere?

CHAPTER 2
Just a Small Town Girl

THERE WAS a distinct smell of perfume in the air as Anaya Mason anxiously glanced at the clock on the back wall of her third-grade classroom at Elmhurst Elementary School. It had been a long semester, and she was finally going to say goodbye to her class at the start of the summer holidays.

Her long brown hair hung loosely down her back, where natural curls formed soft ringlets. With the promise of summer in the air, she'd chosen to wear a light pink satin button-up blouse that accentuated her curves in all the right places. She paired this with a slightly conservative yet still figure-hugging black pencil skirt that sat exactly above her knees.

At thirty years old, Anaya was even more beautiful than she had been growing up. She had a slightly olive complexion, which added to her Mediterranean features. She wore light, neutral-toned eye shadow that emphasized her large brown eyes. The faintest hint of pink lip gloss highlighted her full lips, perfectly proportioning them with her oval face.

A few more minutes, and this long semester would finally

be over! *Am I selfish because I want to do something important for myself for a change? Besides, now is the perfect time to get all those plants for the garden at the church and at home in the ground,* Anaya thought to herself.

She'd been looking forward to these summer holidays for a long time, not just because it meant spending time with her parents, Joe and Diana. She also had several ambitious projects she planned to execute during the holidays. The first was to completely refurbish the nursery in the old chapel, which included some carpentry work, painting, and an entirely new look. Since the beginning, the project had been Anaya's brain-child and would take lots of hard work, but she was adamant about seeing it through.

She wanted to round it all off by planting some colorful foliage and indigenous plants around the entrance to the local Bethlehem Church. Anaya had a heart of gold, and each summer she would find a worthwhile cause to dedicate her time and energy to. This year, it was the church's turn to receive a completely new look.

At long last, the final bell rang for the beginning of the summer holidays. Anaya greeted each of her third-grade students, ensuring they'd each taken their progress reports with them. She would always get them to decorate the large envelope that contained all their artwork for the semester. After helping the last of her students collect their belongings, she finally locked her class, which won't be opened until the beginning of the fall semester in a few months.

Opening her large diary that she carried everywhere, she quickly scanned over her "To-Do List" for the remainder of the day. First, she needed to stop at a fabric shop to look for some gingham fabric suitable for new curtains for the nursery windows. Next was the bookstore, which was within walking distance. That was the beauty of living in Elmhurst. Almost everything was within walking distance when it came to the main shopping centers.

This meant that you could park in a central location and quickly get to each of the retail stores. Scratching the word "fabric" from her list, Anaya looked for some age-appropriate books. The Tattered Book Store sold both old and new books. Anaya spent a fair amount of time going through their books and making a varied selection for the nursery.

It was almost 3:30 p.m., and she had arranged to meet up with Sam Chapman, Kase's older brother, at the Saffron Diner on Main Street. The diner was someplace she and Kase used to spend time quite often, and this connection wasn't lost on Sam at all. He read Anaya like a book but wasn't prepared to let her in on that.

Anaya had chosen to sit at the booth where she and Kase always used to sit. Sam never missed a beat as he noticed how sad and lonely Anaya was, even though she always had a smile on her face. Behind her large brown eyes, Sam could see a decade's worth of regret.

At thirty-six years old, Sam had similar sandy-colored hair to Kase, but that was as far as their similarity went. Sam was a few inches shorter than his brother. What had once been the solid frame of a high school football player had now turned into a softer, cuddlier version. Married and family life seemed to agree with Sam.

"Hi there, Sam. How are you and the family keeping?" Anaya greeted him, kissing him on each side of his cheeks. They had known each other forever, and it seemed like she was more of a sister than Kase's ex-girlfriend.

"The boys are great; just really excited for the summer vacation. They're going to drive us insane! They have so many activities planned and are looking forward to the summer festival. By the time we get to the end of summer, we'll need another holiday," he quipped in his typical jovial manner.

"How is Julie doing? The baby must be due pretty soon? That's so exciting for all of you." Anaya referred to Sam's wife, who was seven months pregnant with their third child, a little girl.

Anaya loved hearing about people who were starting families all around her. Nonetheless, it made her feel even more alone than she already was. Not only was Anaya miles away from starting a family, but it was also pretty much impossible because she wasn't even dating. In some ways, she was even jealous of each of these women as she thought about the life she could have had and how her current life was slipping away from her.

"Julie has her ups and downs. This pregnancy has been different. I think it's because it's a girl, and you women are all alike," Sam teased Anaya. "She can't wait for it to all to be over, but then the pajama parade starts. I guess then it's my turn." Sam was always a bit quirky and fun-loving.

Anaya was comfortable talking with Sam and his family because she felt that this way, she could have a little piece of Kase with her. The last thing she'd ever do was actually ask about him. She got to know Sam and Julie quite well when their son, Ethan, was in her third-grade class. Anaya missed Kase more than she would ever let on to anyone. While she had many eligible suitors lining up outside her door, not one of them had managed to make it to a first date.

"Sam, I desperately need your help with some renovation work at the church. You're the only one I know that has some carpentry experience..." she trailed off, stopping herself from bringing up Kase in their conversation.

"Sure, Anaya, what do you need to be done? You know that I'm always happy to help when it comes to the church." Sam and his family were faithful members of the congregation at Bethlehem Church. If Julie wasn't heavily pregnant, he would have been there, volunteering right alongside her.

"Shelves need to be measured and made to fit in the space available, and then there's some painting that needs to be done too," Anaya explained.

"Should we meet to go over what you need in the morning?" Sam smiled broadly. He'd always been kind and fun to be around, even when she was dating Kase.

"Sure, I'll give you a call a bit later to confirm whether we can get into the church." With that, Anaya excused herself.

Leaving the diner, a sense of sadness set in. It hit Anaya that she was likely to end up an old maid—unmarried and with no children. This briefly reminded her of some of her senior school teachers that she'd had growing up in Elmhurst, who suffered the same fate. That was why they became schoolteachers. The children were a daily substitute for their own children. Was this why she became a schoolteacher in the first place?

Her jealousy was her own doing. Although she was constantly receiving a steady stream of invitations from eligible bachelors, each was declined and promptly sent packing as though they were door-to-door salesmen. There really was only one name that could ever find its way into her heart, and that was Kase.

Nobody would ever be able to replace him, and she would probably love him until the day she died. Was she unreasonable? In ten years, he had never returned to Elmhurst. Hell, he'd never called or written to her—absolutely nothing. He'd probably moved on long ago.

I was responsible for dumping him after all, she thought. *If only I could have a do-over and explain the situation to him. Why I couldn't leave with him that night. I'm optimistic that he will be more than understanding of the situation. He may even forgive me...* Anaya caught herself in the middle of this thought, reasoning that she needed to get what she figured were unrealistic fantasies under control.

Thinking about Kase, over time, became a regular occurrence for Anaya. Despite her previous resolution, she wondered what he was doing at this exact moment.

CHAPTER 3
Still a Hometown Boy

THE CHAPMEN HAVE LIVED in Elmhurst their whole lives. The only one to ever decide to pursue a career outside of the sleepy little town was Kase. Isaac and Susan lived in a beautiful Victorian-style, double-story home on the outskirts of Elmhurst. Most of the houses and buildings on that side of town had been declared heritage sites. They needed to be maintained according to strict building codes and special guidelines. The front of the house had a semi-enclosed porch running along the front of the house.

It was nestled among several large pacific willow trees that provided beautiful shade in summer and protected the home against the harsh elements of winter. Large bay windows look out over a lush green lawn that was immaculately trimmed to perfection by Isaac. Susan had always been a stay-at-home mom, and once Kase left home, what had just been a gardening hobby became an obsession. Her ability to work with different colors and plant varieties could be appreciated all around the perimeter of their home.

The house had been in the Chapman family for several generations. Isaac and Susan were constantly working to maintain the integrity of the home structure as a heritage site. However, it still had plenty of modern conveniences on the inside.

Part of the reason why Jack chose to return home for his month-long prescribed sabbatical was not only because Elmhurst was in the middle of nowhere but also because Isaac was the town doctor at the local clinic. Should anything happen to him during this time, he knew he would be in good hands.

This was the first time that Kase was returning home to Elmhurst since he'd turned off Main Street onto Route 211 while watching the town disappear in a blaze of glory via his rearview mirrors. Just over ten years before, he fought back the tears with hundreds of questions fighting one another for dominance in his brain. Why had she suddenly dumped him? There had been no warning, and Kase felt utterly betrayed.

Besides being more athletic than Sam while growing up, Kase always found himself in trouble. He had earned the reputation of being a bit of a wild child. Although he had put on this bad boy persona for the rest of the world, Anaya got to know the real Kase Chapman. The one that was absolutely different around her.

Susan had always been at home to assist Sam and Kase with their schoolwork, transporting them to activities. She worked on the parent's committee, helped with fundraisers, and was a pillar of strength in the community.

No wonder people often wondered what the hell happened to Kase. With such perfect parents and a perfect brother to boot, it was difficult for Kase to live up to the family's reputation, and why should he? He was his own person and needed to make his own indelible mark on the world.

Since he was a senior and young Anaya Mason, that had been the plan since he was in the seventh grade.

It was his first night home; having flown into Arcata, California, airport, Kase arranged a top-of-the-line F350 truck as a hire vehicle to drive the thirty miles to Elmhurst. Driving back on Route 211, all he could think about was Anaya.

Things will likely be very awkward... with any luck, she has found someone else and moved on from Elmhurst. It will be painful to see her with someone else, but hopefully she's happy.

Arriving shortly after 3:00, Kase managed to have a quick shower and a very brief catch-up with his parents. He didn't see his way clear to having to explain himself twice in one night, given that Sam and his family would be joining them for an early dinner.

The entire family was so excited to see him after ten years. Sam introduced his wife, Julie, whom Kase instantly liked. Kase got a grand tour of the house from his nephews, who ultimately just wanted a ride in the shiny new truck parked in the driveway!

Susan had cooked his family favorite, roast beef with baby potatoes, corn on the cob with baby peas, and julienne carrots. For dessert, they would have ice cream with hot chocolate sauce. The meal instantly reminded Kase of his happier days when he was at home. It had been a long time since he last enjoyed a home-cooked meal. He found himself reminiscing over days gone by.

"Mom, this has been delicious as usual. You have no idea what I'd give for some plain, good old-fashioned home-style cooking."

"How long do you get to stay, Kase?" Susan asked her son. From their communication over the years, he'd always been too busy to get away, let alone come home for a visit.

"Well, there's good news and there's bad news, depending on how you want to look at it. The good news is that I'm going to be here for a month."

"And the bad news?" Isaac interjects.

"Ah... no communication is allowed between me and the outside world at all. I had to leave my laptop, phones, and all other electronic devices in Vegas. According to the casino doctor, I may have a problem with my heart, and I need some serious downtime. This month needs to be totally unplugged. Don't ask me how I'm going to survive not knowing what's going on in each of the casinos, but I just have to trust that they're each in the best possible hands for now."

The tension and concern around the dinner table could be cut with a knife. The family knew that Kase was probably one of the hardest workers they'd ever meet. Whatever this was, it must have been pretty serious to warrant such a long recovery time. Isaac was especially concerned for his son. He was at least assured that he knew what to look for while Kase would be at home.

"Well, we'll just have to try and help you stay off of anything digital during your time here. You were told to forget about the casinos, so that's what we're going to do."

"Beer Kase? Let's go and have a chat outside on the porch. When last did you watch a real Elmhurst sunset?" Sam offered him an ice-cold beer, and Kase had to admit that he'd begun to feel more relaxed than he'd been in a long time.

"I can't believe that you're married and all domesticated, Sam! You and Julie look very happy together, though; marriage looks good on you! I really take my hat off to you. I don't know if I will ever be able to settle down with the kind of life you've chosen for you and your family." Kase felt he needed to clarify his point. "It's not that there's no honor in the way that you've settled down and what you're doing, because clearly, it's working. All you have to do is take a look at Ethan and Joshua and the relationship you have with Julie to realize that you made the right decision for you. I'm so proud of you, Sam!" Kase hugged his brother out of genuine admiration.

"Uncle Kase, Uncle Kase, you promised we could see inside the truck after dinner." Ethan and Joshua were typical young boys eager to see inside a brand-new F350. Allowing them to explore, he returned to his beer and his brother on the porch.

He had to admit he liked the sound of being called Uncle Kase—it had a nice ring to it.

Kase had never really spent time with Julie when they were growing up. He vaguely remembered her as a pretty blonde girl who was of average height and build. She seemed fun to be around, and she and Sam made a great couple.

"Kase, it's not too late, you know..." Sam began but decided not to go any further.

"I'm just not this small-town guy anymore. Don't know if I ever was, really. You know that the casino and gaming industry is everything I ever dreamed it would be and more. I can't explain the instant rush of adrenaline at the start of each new day."

Sam could see that Kase had taken to the gaming industry like a duck to water, and this trip was going to be like tossing the duck into a desert.

Kase deliberately chose to leave out how stressful it was owning and managing multiple casinos. He especially left out all the parts about the embezzlement at the Silver Palms Salt Lake casino, his heart palpitations, and collapsing in the gym. Nobody needed to hear about that because they'd all just pamper and fuss over him.

"Bro, I've sort of been roped into this community project

that involves some woodwork, shelving, and painting. Why don't you come along with me? It will be good for the two of us to work side by side again. What do you say?"

Kase was a bit suspicious of the way that Sam was so nonchalant about this project. Usually, his brother was extremely particular, right down to the very last detail. Tonight, he seemed to be evasive for some reason. Kase dismissed his suspicions down to the paranoia of everything that happened at the Silver Palms Salt Lake Casino of late and decided to put it at the back of his mind.

"Sure, that sounds great. I'd love to get to work side-by-side with you again!" In truth, Kase was already beginning to feel a bit of cabin fever setting in. He realized he would need to be kept busy for the next month if he planned on keeping his sanity. This project sounded like something he'd enjoy, and his father didn't seem to be against the idea.

He couldn't remember when he last worked with his hands, physically doing woodwork or construction. It was at least ten years ago.

"I hope I remember how to work with most of the equipment." He joked with Sam.

"Just like riding a bicycle, Kase, you'll get back into it in no time at all."

Maybe the fact that it was a "community project" would do something to alleviate Kase's typical bad boy image around Elmhurst for once? He had been gone for just over a decade but was sure that there would still be those who would pick up on it if they discovered he was home. Giving back to the community had to mean something.

Not that he was going to let that stress him out at all—he had more than enough stress with each of the casinos. It was only the first evening, and he was already ready to buy new electronic devices. Just to be able to get in communication with those he'd left in charge at each resort.

Although Kase loved being at home with his family, he had already begun to feel a bit bored and anchored to one place. This was going to be one long-ass month if he had nothing to do. He couldn't remember the last time he'd actually had some serious downtime.

He missed his penthouse apartment, along with everything else in it. In so many ways, Kase was far too spoiled. He was used to all the luxuries and finer things in life that money could afford. He missed most about the penthouse: the space, the privacy, the magnificent views of Vegas cityscapes, and the front of the Vegas strip along with the fountains and Silver Sands Vegas. Kase figured that his parents' entire home could comfortably fit inside his apartment with some room to spare.

Sam excused himself to make a phone call, and Kase soaked in the evening sunset from one of the chairs on the porch.

It had been many years since he had even thought of the sunsets in Elmhurst, unless they featured the gorgeous Miss Anaya Mason! Now, now, Kase, you know that the chances of Anaya even being in Elmhurst anymore are probably as remote as hell.

"That's all confirmed for first thing tomorrow morning. We're going to meet up with the organizer of this whole project. They've agreed to cook us breakfast, so don't worry about having anything here. I'll pick you up at around seven or so?" Sam was still not letting on who this person was. Kase decided to let it slide.

"I probably don't know them anyway, so I'll let tomorrow take care of itself," Kase said.

"Another beer, Sam?"

"Sure, and then that's me. I need to get the family home sometime. Julie is probably already irritated with me because I left her and Mom to do the dishes on their own."

Wow, dishes—Kase seriously couldn't remember a time in

almost a decade where he had to wash a dish. The hotel industry had taught him to be lazy. Maybe that's what he needed over this next month—a couple of life lessons to bring him back down to earth.

CHAPTER 4
The One That Got Away

IT WAS the first day of the summer holidays, and Anaya couldn't have asked for a more glorious morning. The sun rose over the distant mountains, bathing the entire town in different shades of fresh ember. Stretching her arms, she felt excited about getting her project at the church on course. She took a quick shower and slipped into a pair of skin-tight jeans and a skinny t-shirt that clung to her trim waistline but accentuated her large breasts. She took her damp hair and tied it into a long braid behind her back. She felt quite comfortable with how she was dressed, seeing as it was just Sam and another helper he'd managed to convince to work at the church.

Then she got started on cooking some omelets going and brewing fresh coffee. As Anaya had the last of the omelets cooking, she heard Sam's truck pull into her driveway. The timing couldn't be more perfect. Adding the final omelet to the others in the warmer, she threw a dish towel over her shoulder and bounced to answer the door before Sam had the chance to ring the bell.

Her home was built on a hillside and was a comfortable size. It was on the newer side of town, where the houses were smaller but more modern than the heritage homes where both her parents and the Chapmans stayed. The outside of her home had a small covered patio with large pillars at the entrance.

Most of the garden had already been turned and dug up with fertilizer. All they needed now were the flowers she planned on planting there over the summer. Two well-established trees stood in the garden, along with some neatly trimmed hedges leading up to her home's main steps.

Anaya opened the door to Sam, who had a broad grin from ear to ear. She was about to throw her arms around him as she usually would when a familiar yet older figure made himself known from behind Sam. The two locked eyes on each other, and there was complete silence from both of them as they stood there staring at each other in total disbelief. The silence was now beginning to fill the air with a degree of heaviness.

"Sorry, Anaya, I didn't want to ruin the surprise. SURPRISE!" Sam said, motioning to Kase.

There was a total look of shock and horror on both Anaya's and Kase's faces when they realized that they'd just been set up by Sam. Anaya felt as though she must have been dreaming and motioned for them to come inside. She felt as though she would wake up from a pleasant dream any minute, and it would be morning.

Speechless, they stared at each other for a few moments, and then Kase turned on his heels toward his brother. Pulling him to one side and speaking in low enough tones so that Anaya wouldn't hear him, he appeared frustrated.

Anaya wasn't paying the two brothers any attention, though. Her knees suddenly felt wobbly underneath her, despite feeling full of life and energy only a few minutes before answering her front door. She managed to hold onto her kitchen countertop to keep herself steady until she could regain her balance.

"How dare he suddenly show up here out of the blue like this? Batting those hazel eyes at me," she muttered to herself. She wasn't even happy that he was in her home, right in her kitchen, and that she'd actually made breakfast for him. One of the biggest problems Anaya had this morning wasn't that Kase was there at all. It was what he looked like.

As much as Anaya was good at reading Kase ten years ago, she wasn't sure whether she still had that superpower over him. The man had become totally hot! It suddenly dawned on her that the reason for her not moving on was because he was so good-looking—especially those hazel eyes and his firm, square jawline.

What was it about this man that could send this girl completely "gaga" over him? She wasn't some little schoolgirl anymore. She should be able to control the thoughts and emotions she was going feeling right now, shouldn't she? What was unique about this man that put her into a complete tailspin and made her brain turn to mush?

A million different scenarios were playing out in her head right now, and not one of them seemed to end very well for either of them. Her life had been perfect to this point. Why did he have to finally come back to Elmhurst, especially looking like a million bucks in those jeans and that tight t-shirt? She could see his muscles rippling underneath his shirt, and with that, her cheeks became flushed. All she could imagine was being nestled in the safety and security of his arms again.

Dang Anaya, pull yourself together. You cannot let this guy mess with your head right now. There's too much riding on this church project. I don't even think that I can work so close to him on this thing. I'm going to have to think about this between now and the end of breakfast.

"Well, standing here is letting the eggs spoil. Let's eat, guys."

Anaya was not only unhappy that Kase was so close by, but she was also furious that Sam hadn't said anything about Kase's visit the previous day at diner or the previous night when he called. Kase had to have been in Elmhurst all ready for him to be making all these promises. At least she could hide her bit of a blush while she dished up the omelets on individual plates, poured coffee just the way each of the brothers preferred it, and joined them at the kitchen table.

It was the first time she really got a good look at Kase, and he seemed extremely angry at her. She couldn't blame him. It was a pity that he was still as handsome as ever, just as she'd imagined he would be, maybe even more. The years had been good to Kase. Perhaps it was just the easy lifestyle that he got to lead that kept him looking so fit and healthy.

Stop it, Anaya! You can see that he's so over you; it's just not funny. No wedding ring, although what does that actually prove? He was living the high life in all the casinos, from what she had heard about him. He was probably married with kids already. She was still not sure how she felt about him being in her kitchen right now.

Breakfast was eaten in absolute silence between Anaya and Kase. Sam tried to get a conversation started and flowing without much luck at all.

"Kase is only too happy to help me with the church for you," Sam announced.

"That's not necessary. I can handle everything on my own, thank you!" Anaya retorted.

"Well, that's fine by me. I'm here to rest in any event, so

not helping out works for me too!" Kase said, placing his knife and fork together on the plate. Kase was noticeably hurt by her remarks, something that Anaya picked up on.

There's so much history between us, I really wouldn't know where to begin. I hurt him again this morning. Why can't you just keep quiet and allow other people in? This is Kase that we're talking about, not Jack the Ripper. What the hell's gotten into you? It seems like he's going to be in town for a while. You will probably have to come clean with him at some point regarding what actually happened ten years ago and what the real reason for everything was. Anaya thought to herself.

They had planned everything down to the very last detail to run away together so Kase could follow his dream of making a name for himself in Vegas. First, they'd agreed to go through a typical Vegas-style wedding. Kase was so afraid of Joe Mason back in the day that he could never seem to pluck up the courage to formally ask him for Anaya's hand in marriage.

Kase knew that this was why Joe didn't like him very much. He was well aware that Jim thought that Kase was no good—a misfit in society who had no real future ahead of him other than possibly in a local penitentiary. Kase had been blaming Jim all these years for getting through to Anaya and convincing her that she would be throwing her life away if she dared run away with Kase.

The truth was that Anaya had already packed up her belongings and was ready to meet up with Kase at their special spot when she received an urgent call from an oncologist at the local hospital. Her mother had just been diagnosed with breast cancer, and they weren't sure whether she was going to make it.

Her mother's condition was already at stage 3, which was quite advanced and needed surgery almost immediately to remove the tumors. Then it would be radiation and chemotherapy if they were going to be confident that they had it all under control. It was going to be touch and go for quite a while in the Mason home, and she didn't want to do anything to negatively impact Kase's dream of doing great things in Vegas.

Unfortunately, the predicament of her mom's cancer couldn't have come at a worse time. There were so many nights that Anaya would cry herself to sleep, torn between her decision to stay and nurse her mother through cancer or join Kase in Vegas.

She'd written so many letters to Kase over the years, trying to articulate on paper precisely what had happened and explaining to him that her feelings for him had never changed. Of course, none of these letters ever made it past the draft stage. Anaya was just as afraid of how he would react to the news about her mom.

Knowing Kase, though, he would have turned around and come home to help Nurse Diana Mason back to health.

Her mom's recovery had been prolonged and painful. This was because she had some severe reactions to both the chemotherapy and radiation therapies being used. This meant that the oncologists could only treat her with extremely low dosages of all the chemicals. Naturally, the overall effect was much slower than they'd all hoped for.

What was the point of trying to explain all of this to him now? The past is in the past, and that's probably where it should stay. Returning to the present,

"Sam, I don't think you need to bother either. I think you've done enough for this project. I'll manage on my own," Anaya added.

Accepting the tone in Anaya's voice as an indication for them to leave, both Sam and Kase left their coffee half empty and sheepishly walked out of her home.

CHAPTER 5
Oh, Cupid!

"WHAT THE HELL did you go and do that for?" Kase turned his full-blown anger on his brother. "Do you have any idea how awkward I felt there, sitting in her kitchen, when we haven't said two words to each other in over a decade?" That blood vessel on his forehead was beginning to pulsate, as it usually does whenever he gets agitated.

"Well, maybe it's about time that both of you grow up and start talking with each other. I think that you might just find it to be enlightening." Sam just shrugged his shoulders nonchalantly and kept on driving.

"Sam, I'm telling you that you're fortunate that you're my brother and also that I don't know what's happening with this heart of mine right now. Otherwise, I can promise you that we would have had this out just like the old days!" Kase referred to them settling petty disputes and squabbles when they were teenagers by sparring it out in the boxing ring. Needless to say, Kase always seemed to win.

"What the hell were you thinking? You know, as far as I'm

concerned, Anaya is the very last person I wanted to or needed to see on this trip back home!"

"Let's face it, though, if I had told you we were going to Anaya's house this morning, would you have agreed to come with me?" Sam made a very valid argument, but Kase was still seething.

He had to admit that she had grown into such a beautiful woman—even more beautiful than when they were planning on eloping together. Despite looking beautiful, from what he'd managed to see briefly this morning, there was something sad about her. Her eyes betrayed her, as usual. Did she have regrets for not running away with him? His mind was now filled with more questions than answers.

"I'm really sorry if you thought I did this to hurt you. I just really figured that it was time the two of you had a reunion! Don't you think it's time to bury the knives?" Sam sounded serious as he dropped his brother back at their parents' home.

"Sam, do I really need to remind you that she was the one who dumped me? It wasn't the other way around..."

"Maybe it's time that you actually sit down and really talk to her. Find out why she never followed you instead of trying to work through all these conclusions you've been jumping to for the last decade."

Kase's mind was spinning and spinning. He did want to know why Anaya never showed up. She didn't have a ring on her finger, which has to be a good sign. Maybe she hasn't been able to move on either. Does Sam know more about this than he's letting on? He was awfully pushy; it's like he knows something *about what happened that I don't. Why can't people just be upfront and honest instead of insisting on playing all these mind games?* He thought.

Kase spent the rest of the day lounging around, catching

up with his folks, and helping Isaac with some minor repairs that needed to be taken care of around the home.

When Susan called everyone together for dinner, Kase found himself pushing his chicken fillet around the plate. He had lost his appetite completely. Even though he tried to keep himself busy, his thoughts kept drifting over to Anaya. Even breakfast had been a challenge, as he was feeling nauseous and excited at the same time. He couldn't get her out of his head, and this was not going to do his heart any good. He could feel his pulse racing, just thinking about her.

"I'm sorry, Mom, I'm just not that hungry today. Please excuse me. I think I'm going to try and get some exercise before I turn in for the night!"

It would be easy for Susan to dismiss this as worry over his casinos. It couldn't be easy for him to suddenly be uprooted like that, only to be isolated in the middle of nowhere, which was probably so far out of his current comfort zone. She appeared to accept this but kept her thoughts to herself as she excused Kase from the table.

Kase put on his sneakers and his running gear and decided to head out on a trail that was not too far from his parents' home. It was a trail that he used to run regularly while growing up. He needed to go for a run to clear his mind, which was heading in a thousand different directions all at once.

Kase's feet automatically took him to his and Anaya's favorite spot close to the town's waterfall. It was ten years ago. He and Anaya had met earlier in the day to confirm all their arrangements. She was so excited, and they were both so madly in love with each other. They had been an item since Anaya was in the seventh grade, although if you were to ask either of them, they would tell you it lasted longer than that.

They had grown up together, and Kase and Anaya shared absolutely everything. They told each other everything. They would spend every spare moment together so that they could manage to get away from Joe's disapproval. This was the reason for them finding "their spot" at the town's lake. Most people didn't realize that if you actually swam through the waterfall, there was another entirely secluded, secret lake there.

This was their secret. It had been for years. They would often make their way to the lake under the guise of going for a swim in it. There were always a lot of people there. Kase and Anaya would simply swim through to the other side and enjoy total privacy in the mirrored lake.

They had met up to discuss all their final plans to elope that evening. Kase had made up his mind to get the hell out of Elmhurst. There was no future for him there other than Anaya, and seeing that she was prepared to risk it all and join him made him the happiest man in the world.

Kase would have spoken with Joe Mason to formally ask him for Anaya's hand in marriage, but he knew that the pastor had it out for him for some reason. He went along with his rant, making the rest of the town believe that Kase was basically a misfit in society. Kase wasn't prepared to get into a mud-slinging match with Joe Mason purely because he knew it would hurt Anaya greatly.

Everything was planned. They were in their secret lake when Kase pulled a much younger Anaya close to him, hugging her close. He whispered in her ear in a deep, throaty voice as he was so nervous...

"Miss Anaya Mason, will you do me the honor of becoming Mrs. Chapman? You know that it's only you that I've ever cared about or will care about—what do you say?"

Anaya just nodded with a blush, and they shared a tender kiss while still in the water. Anaya would have done anything for Kase; he was her one true love and her soulmate, or at least that was what she had told him.

Leaving the lake at 5 p.m., Kase dropped Anaya off at home and confirmed that he would see her at 9 that evening back at the lake. Everyone else would be too busy with the summer festival to even notice they had gone. By then, it would be too late. Kase had used all his savings to buy two one-way tickets to Vegas. His dream was to make a name for himself and work his way up to the top as quickly as possible. That would be after he'd made Anaya his wife.

Leaving a little earlier than planned, Kase arrived at the lake at around 7:30 p.m. He decided to get comfortable—but not too comfortable because Anaya would have been arriving anytime soon. Shifting positions in the car, he kept a lookout for Anaya, where they'd agreed to meet. Looking at his watch, it was already 8:30 p.m. *What was taking her so long?* He wondered.

Kase was starting to lose it by 10 p.m., an hour after the time they should have left. He called the airline to reschedule their tickets, realizing that something must have happened. Was she really doing this to him? Could she be that shallow that she would agree to marry him in one breath and skip out on him in the next?

Kase felt extremely worried. He would take a quick swing by the Summer Festival and see if Anaya was there. If not, he had made up his mind that she was sending a signal that was being received loud and clear—she didn't really love him or want to spend the rest of her life with him. The summer festival was still in full swing. As many people as Kase could find, he asked whether anyone had seen Anaya that night. The answer from everyone was no.

Resigning himself to the fact that he had been stood up by Anaya, probably thanks to Joe Mason, Kase decided it was time to hit the road and head down Main Street until he reached Route 211. Fighting back the tears, he was determined to try and process this and vowed he would never let himself be drawn into such a deep love ever again.

Kase's thoughts were quickly brought back to the present

as he realized he'd run much further up the trail than he'd initially planned. He turned around and started heading for his parents' home. Realizing that he needed answers from Anaya, he decided to help her with the church after all. Once he'd showered after his run, he gave Sam a call...

"Sam, I've decided that I'm going to try to help Anaya with the church after all. I know she said she didn't need the help anymore, but I have too many questions, and only she has the answers. Maybe this way, I can finally get some closure." Kase volunteering to help Anaya was exactly what Sam had hoped for.

"I'll pick you up at eight. We can go to the church together."

CHAPTER 6
The Same Old Gang

It was another beautiful summer morning, and Anaya decided to stop by her parent's home on the way to the church. Her mother, Diana Mason, was beginning to show her age. The color of her natural tresses used to be dark brown, and Anaya had inherited her brunette curls. Diana's hair was increasingly beginning to reveal additional streaks of gray.

"Let's organize a girl's trip to the salon sometime over the summer holidays. Mom, we can get that gray in your hair taken care of! My treat..." Anaya offers.

"Thank you, my darling child. I don't mind the gray so much anymore. I've gotten used to it, and in many ways, I'm just thankful to have any hair left at all." Diana answered more humbly than she would have several years ago. Her illness made her acutely aware of the value of life and the importance of living every possible moment to the fullest.

Diana realized that Anaya made had monumental sacrifices to be with her and to nurse her back to good health. She just wished that her daughter would now spend some time looking for that special someone that everyone deserved. Since the day that Kase Chapman left town, Anaya hadn't quite been the same.

Diana had become much frailer over the last decade. The first three to four years had been the worst to deal with. She was eternally grateful to have her daughter around to support her in every possible way. The cancer had taught Diana to view life differently and to live every day as if it were her last.

Anaya and Joe were the most essential people in Diana's life. Anaya's decisions at that time had been the price of happiness and possibly even freedom away from the tiny town of Elmhurst.

When Diana was first diagnosed with cancer, she had never really discussed things with Anaya and wasn't entirely sure whether she would even be honest about it. The ultra-low doses of chemo and radiation had stretched out her treatment period, and it had only been two years since she was declared cancer-free.

Joe was just pleased to finally have his wife back again after so many years of fighting and trips to and from doctors and hospitals. There were many times when he had been touched to go with Diana, and Joe had also relied heavily on his daughter for support. The total cost of this decision was only now beginning to become fully apparent.

Before her diagnosis ten years ago, Diana had a responsible and pressurized bookkeeping job. She was forced to leave all of this behind as soon as her mother's condition was diagnosed. It had been a long, uphill struggle. Nonetheless, through her faith, Joe's encouragement, and Anaya's continued support, she had finally managed to pull through.

Joe Mason had been the pastor at Bethlehem Church for as long as Anaya could remember. His dedication to serving the community was something he was always well known for. Joe would often play the "you're the pastor's daughter" card with Anaya, guilt-tripping her into choosing to live by his set of rules. To a large extent, she was still living under the same circumstances. Joe was still trying to set her up with members of the congregation, but Anaya wasn't falling for it.

Joe and Diana lived in a simple Victorian-style home with a large walkway, stairs, and entrance to the front door. Each of the windows had shutters reminiscent of the period, and the front door had a large ornate door frame. The roof had shingles that glistened in the bright sunlight. The garden was neat enough, but it was easy to tell it had been missing a woman's touch for several years. Anaya had inherited her mother's soft nature and love of gardening and working with plants.

"Hey, Mom and Dad, I'm not planning on staying too long. I thought I would quickly stop in and see how you are both doing on my way down to the church this morning. Is there anything you need from town while I'm there?" This was typical of Anaya with her parents—some may have even called her a "people pleaser", but only when it came to her parents. Her mother gave her a hug and a kiss.

"Are you going down to the church to begin working on your project from today already?" Diana asked her daughter. "I will make something for everyone to eat and bring it down to the church a bit later. How does that sound?"

Anaya didn't have the heart to tell her that she would be the only one working at the church. Instead, she just nodded, trying to figure out what to say once her mom arrived with a selection of food to feed an army. Bless her, she always wanted to be as helpful as she possibly could be, yet this cancer had taken most of the fight out of her.

"I'll be coming down to the church a bit later as well to go through my sermon for Sunday," Joe announced. Anaya was beginning to regret telling the Chapman brothers that she no longer needed their help.

"That's just great! I look forward to seeing both of you a

bit later at the church." Her response didn't sound convincing.

Anaya's thoughts were spiraling over the sudden surprise visit from Kase. She didn't want to tell her mom and dad that she was the only one working at the church since she'd asked Sam not to show. More importantly, she wouldn't be telling her parents that Kase was in town.

She needed to do absolutely everything in her power to keep them apart. Not that Kase was the church-going type at all, so she was probably relatively safe on that front. She knew that there was a seed of animosity between her father and Kase.

Joe had never felt that Kase was good enough for his little girl, and then there was that whole wild child image that Kase had while he was growing up. Anaya still had no clue where that came from because, to her, Kase had been mischievous but never quite wild. Totally lost in thought as she headed over to the church, she was totally blown away to find both Kase and Sam there waiting for her.

"First things first, Kase, come and help me measure here... Anaya, what exactly did you have in mind with these shelves, and where do you want to put them?" Sam wasn't afraid of jumping straight in. This was typical of Sam and one of the reasons Anaya wanted his help. She had absolutely no doubt that whatever Sam was responsible for would be delivered at the highest possible quality and in the quickest possible time.

Sam ran his own carpentry, woodworking, and upholstery business in Elmhurst. He was often known as "Mr. Fix-It". If anyone had something that was broken, Sam was the person they had on speed dial to come and fix it for them.

Kase helped his brother measure the shelves and the three of them discussed precisely the vision that Anaya had for the nursery. This was going to take quite a bit of work, which neither of the Chapmen was afraid of. By most accounts, this was why Kase was home in the first place. Within a few minutes, the two brothers had measured and calculated what supplies they needed and how much. They'd made some notes and a couple of rough sketches in Sam's diary that he carried around with him.

"I suggest that we all go for the supplies. That way, you get to choose the type of wooden finish you would like, Anaya, as well as the different color paints. There are several things we're going to need out of the church budget. I'm willing to help with all the tools and labor." Sam believed in rolling up his sleeves and getting right down to business.

Fortunately, Anaya agreed. Despite the fact that she was scared of letting these two men go and select paint for a nursery that needed to be inviting for the children, she trusted them implicitly when it came to selecting the woods that needed to be purchased. In addition to this, she had the funds for all the materials they needed to purchase.

The three climbed into Sam's truck and started heading down Main Street to Elmhurst's hardware store. On their way there, Kase asked if they could stop at the café. This just so happened to be the very same café where he and Anaya shared their first kiss. Anaya and Kase exchanged several looks. Kase's cheeks were slightly flushed, matching the same color as Anaya's.

He couldn't help remembering what her soft, full lips felt like on that summer afternoon. It was anything but an ordinary day. For Kase, it would be one of the most memorable days of his life.

He had convinced the young girl of his dreams to go steady with him. His young sixteen-year-old heart fluttered. Still a bit awkward around fourteen-year-old Anaya, he'd had his eye on her ever since he could remember.

She'd finally decided to give him a bit of a break and chose to believe in him rather than the rumor mill that was Elmhurst at the time. That was the problem with small towns. Everyone knew everyone's business.

Kase knew that Anaya was also thinking about that very first kiss and how things would never be the same for her ever again. Quickly trying to break the silence, Kase made the first move.

"How are your parents, Anaya? I really hope that I'll get to see them while I'm still here."

"They're doing great, thanks. You may still get to see them this afternoon at the church. Mom is bringing some food over, and Dad wants to go over his sermon for Sunday." The color of her cheeks was returning to normal.

"How are things in the big city? You still in Vegas?" she asked.

"Vegas is incredible! I don't think I could ask for anything more than I have right now," Kase lied. He knew that the one thing that would make his life way more bearable would be if Anaya was there with him... His thoughts were interrupted by Sam.

"Now that you two have had your blast from the past session, can we get to the hardware store?" They both burst into laughter—it had been more than a decade since that last happened. In all the time that Kase and Anaya had been dating, Sam had been around most of the time. He was like a big-brother chaperone.

This gave Kase far more freedom with his parents. They actually trusted Sam way more than they did Kase, which was the reason why the three became almost inseparable. Sam gave Kase and Anaya the space they needed for their young love to blossom. He had played an active part in the success of their relationship.

Getting the old "gang" together again felt comfortable for

each of them, despite the personal differences between Anaya and Kase. Sam knew that if he gave them enough time and space, they would definitely be able to make their way back to each other. The only other love that he'd seen that was that strong was the love he and Julie shared.

CHAPTER 7
Mr. Wrong?

FOR THE FIRST time in ages, Anaya and Kase were working alongside each other once again. Sam and Kase cut the lumber needed to build the shelving, while Anaya worked on taping the walls to prep for the painting. Several ladies from the church congregation had stopped by to help Anaya. While Anaya was busy with the women's assistance, Sam decided to tackle Kase's plans regarding Anaya.

"So, when are you going to make your move? I can see it written all over your face again, Kase, you are still totally awestruck by this woman! If you're only here for a month, I don't suggest that you leave it too long. She's still so in love with you. It's scary, man!"

"You know that I've never stopped loving her, Sam, not even after she dumped me like that with no reason. I've tried to stay mad at her, but seeing her again after all these years, it all seems pretty futile. How do you propose this working out for us, Sam? Do you not think that I've been thinking along these same lines ever since you hijacked me to trick us into meeting each other? You sneaky bastard!"

45

"How do you know she doesn't feel exactly the same way about you? You know that she's never dated anyone else since you left!"

"You can't be serious? Nobody?" Kase looked at his brother, totally dumbstruck. "But she's so beautiful, maybe even more so than when we were still teenagers. She's had plenty of time to come and look for me or to write to me. Hell, all she had to do was make a couple of calls around Vegas. Everyone knows who I am and usually where I am at any given time. She could have called or even written—nothing! How does that translate into her liking me?"

Who in their right mind would be prepared to let someone who was so funny, compassionate, and just an all-around amazing woman slip through their fingers?

Their conversation was cut short as Diana Mason arrived with lunch. Kase was really pleased to see her, and she gave him a hug. He could tell that there was something wrong with Diana immediately. She'd lost a lot of weight since Kase last saw her, and she looked much older than he knew she was. She'd also lost a bit of the mischievous sparkle in her eyes that allowed her and Kase to connect so well. Before Kase could ask her if she was okay, Joe Mason showed up to check on the progress of the work. He was clearly shocked to see Kase and almost did a double-take.

"When did you show up?"

"I've been in town for a couple of days now..."

"Why have you come back now? Where have you been all this time? And how long are you planning on staying in town?" the pastor interrupted him before he could get another word in.

Joe Mason clearly wasn't happy that Anaya's old boyfriend was back in town.

Joe had never approved of Kase as a suitable match for his daughter. He didn't like him when he was a child because he was always getting into trouble. His major gripe with Kase was that he didn't have the guts to ask him for Anaya's hand in marriage. Thank goodness Anaya had dodged that bullet. When he heard that they had planned to elope together, Joe almost lost the plot completely. He thought that Kase was completely spineless and a bad influence on Anaya. The sooner he got back out of town and away from Anaya, the better.

"Well, I'm actually home under strict orders from my doctor that I get some rest. I will probably be here for about a month in total and will then be returning to Vegas."

"Are you okay?" Anaya gasped, genuinely concerned about Kase, as Joe's tact finally got the better of him.

Her concern made Kase realize that maybe she genuinely still cared about him—not that it would do him any good, especially not now. He was responsible for eight of the largest casinos all across the US. There was no way he could run an operation like that from Elmhurst. Besides, in the few days he'd been there, he'd already suffered from extreme cabin fever. While the quaint little out-of-the-way town held a certain charm for tourists and those wanting to drive through and appreciate a small town rich in Victorian era heritage, Elmhurst had this in bucket loads. It wasn't somewhere that a highly successful entrepreneur would be able to run a multi-billion-dollar gaming operation from.

Why are you even thinking about this, Kase? You already know what the answer is. There is no chance that Anaya will even come away with you for a few days once this forced sabbatical has come to an end. How crazy are you to even think that she would even consider coming with you a second time? Kase caught himself and his overactive imagination that was running away with him.

"I'm fine, thanks; it's just work-related anxiety from being busy and dealing with loads of stressful situations."

"Maybe you should be taking things easy? You really don't need to help out here at the church, especially if you are meant to be resting." There was genuine concern in her voice.

"Believe me, if this starts becoming too much to handle, I will let you know, I promise!"

"I think that's it for today. Let's just tidy up quickly. Tomorrow is another day."

As they were packing away, they reached for the ladder simultaneously, and their hands made contact. Immediately, it was like a bolt of lightning through each of them. Whatever they had in the past was definitely still there, no doubt about it. Kase was perplexed. He definitely felt exactly the same chemistry they shared ten years earlier.

As they were leaving, Anaya was about to get into her car when she stopped and called after Kase.

"Hey, can we talk?" She asked him as they were getting ready to leave for the day. "I mean, like, go somewhere and talk."

He definitely wanted to talk, but where would that lead their relationship, especially when he left again?

She was firmly established in the town, in her home—but one look into those deep brown eyes, and he had no option but to say yes!

Right now, it seemed Anaya was in the driver's seat, leading the way in whatever direction this relationship appeared to be heading. Kase felt like he was a passenger being dragged along for the ride, and the ride seemed to be getting more and more enjoyable.

CHAPTER 8
Bittersweet Memories

"LET'S meet at our old spot. I know it's a bit out of the way, but you know how pretty it can be as the sun goes down." This was somewhere that the two of them would hang out and make out like teenagers. It was their own private spot.

Parking on the outskirts of the lake, Anaya climbed into Kase's truck for them to have a full-blown, honest, heart-to-heart conversation about what had really happened ten years ago.

"How are you enjoying working in the casino business?" Anaya started the conversation.

"It's good. A huge success, actually. There are some days when I still can't believe how quickly I managed to make it in this business or become as successful as I have in a relatively short time." Kase looked as though he was in pain while sharing this information with her. "Truth is, Anaya, this had always been something that I thought you and I were going to be sharing together. I cannot tell you how many times I think about you, and only you, whenever there's something to celebrate."

Finally coming clean, Anaya decided to break her silence.

"Kase, that night that we were meant to be leaving for Vegas, I really think I owe you a major explanation for what happened that day and night. I was totally packed and ready to come and meet you when I received a phone call from the hospital, asking me to meet my parents there," she recounted. There was sadness in her voice as she continued to recollect her experiences that night. "My parents were meant to be at the Summer Festival, and I wasn't expecting to have to go to the hospital. When I arrived, my mom and dad were already sitting there with Dr. Byrne. He explained that my mom had stage 3 breast cancer and needed to surgery immediately." Anaya was still very emotional about it, and the memory seemed too painful for her to bear. She continued.

"The doctor confirmed that if she didn't have the operation immediately to remove the tumors they'd found, then she probably only had a few months left to live. They operated on her that night, Kase. When I was supposed to be meeting with you, I was praying for my mother's life at the local hospital," she added.

"Oh, Anaya, why didn't you just call me? Why didn't you let me know what was going on? I could have been here this whole time helping you!"

"That was exactly why I didn't call you, Kase. You had this amazing dream to go to Vegas and make something for yourself. How could I possibly expect you to be willing to give up on what you'd been working so hard on for so long?"

"Yes, but Vegas could have waited for a couple of months!"

"That was the thing, though. Once they started with the chemo and radiation, Mom got so ill from the doses. The whole treatment regimen changed for her. What should have only taken her a few months to get over and be declared cancer-free took several years instead. In between taking care of both my mom and my dad, I needed to find work, and the safest bet when it came to employment was to become a teacher." Her voice trailed off in the distance, and Kase could pick up on regret if he ever heard it.

"Oh, Anaya," Kase said as he wrapped his arms around her. For the first time in ten years, she felt safe and secure back in Kase's arms, where she knew she belonged. "I thought our love was strong enough for this. Why didn't you tell me?"

Kase remembered a time when they would share absolutely everything with each other, going all the way back to high school. They'd shared very personal information about their hopes and dreams and vowed never to keep any secrets. It had worked out perfectly up until the night they were supposed to leave.

"There was no way I could ever have asked you to give up your dream of making something of yourself in Vegas," she told him.

"Yeah, Anaya, but that wasn't your decision to make. I could have postponed it for a while, and it wouldn't have impacted me negatively. Look at where I am today at just thirty-two!"

"When do you have to go back to Vegas?" she asked the one question that to which she was not too sure whether she wanted to hear the answer.

"Probably once the month is up. I bought another phone here because this radio silence thing is not working for me. Still, I didn't bring any of my contacts, so I can't even get in contact with the casino managers to find out what's happening. The doctor in Vegas wanted me to be totally stress-free by the time I go back." They sat in silence for a while, both reflecting on the moments that had passed.

"Let's go for a walk around the lake. The sunset is really beautiful at this time of the day out here."

Kase agreed, running around and opening the door for her, and then he lifted her out, much like he used to do in the old days. Anaya giggled. They had so many beautiful memories of growing up around the lake, and it was a central part of their love for each other.

They were walking hand in hand, and the conversation became more relaxed between them.

Everything about Diana's health needed to come out, and as Anaya suspected, Kase would have stayed behind to support her. Had she made the wrong decision all those years by not calling him the moment she received the news about her mother?

Not too far from the water's edge, they found a huge willow tree with countless hearts and initials carved into the trunk. It took them a few seconds to find theirs.

"Do you remember this day?" Kase pulled her closer toward him while pushing her back up against the tree.

"Uh-huh" was all that Anaya could manage to say.

"I really want to kiss you right now, Anaya. Is it okay if I do that?"

"Uh-huh..." her answer was almost inaudible because she'd been waiting years for this.

Kase gently leaned in and found her parted lips. The last decade seemed to simply fade away, and they were once again twenty-two and twenty, respectively. She pulled Kase closer by slipping her arms around his neck. Pleasurable memories of the past came flooding back for both of them.

They had often made out against the large willow tree. They could both sense the level of desire for each other increasing rapidly.

Out of respect for Anaya, Kase pulled back, trying desperately to restrain himself.

"Why are you stopping, Kase?" Anaya asked sincerely.

"Where do you see this going, Anaya? I think we both need to be totally realistic here. You are established in Elmhurst, and it's unlikely that you will ever move to Vegas.

Due to the nature of my work, I can't run and manage eight different casinos from Elmhurst. So, where does this leave us?"

"Can't we just enjoy what we have here and now and wait to see what the future holds?"

"You know that's now how I do things, Anaya. It's definitely going to lead to one, or even both, of us getting hurt pretty badly." Kase suddenly paused, as if having a realization. "You're right, Anaya; why don't we just let the situation play out and see where it leads? We've only got everything to lose and nothing to gain right now, but what the heck!"

Anaya really wanted Kase back in her life, but she was just as much of a realist. She knew that she would never be able to leave her home, her family, the school, and her students, all for the love of her life. Or could she?

CHAPTER 9
Feels Like Old Times

FOR THE NEXT TWO DAYS, Anaya and Kase worked closely together in the garden at the church and her garden at home, planting flowers. On the days when they started off in her own garden, Anaya made them omelets for breakfast. The best time for planting was usually in the morning before the summer heat set in for the day. They would then move back to the nursery at the church to continue taping the edges to prepare the walls and door for painting.

They had been used to working on community projects together in high school. And even though Kase still had a reputation that he simply couldn't seem to shake, he was hoping that somehow this would gain him a little bit of favor with the small community in Elmhurst, which never seemed to forgive or forget. Not that Kase had anything to be forgiven for; he was just a typical loud teenager who had big dreams.

Something was bugging Kase about what Anaya had told him about her mom's illness. *Why couldn't she tell me what she was going through with her mother's cancer? I cannot believe she decided to hide that from me and do it alone. This must have been so tough on her. I could have been here for her to help her. Even if that just meant being able to listen and comfort her throughout the process. Why does she always have to be so stubborn? We've always shared absolutely everything, so why did she feel she wasn't able to share this?*

Kase's thoughts were interrupted by a call from Sam.

"Hey, Kase, please let Anaya know that I cannot make it to the church today to help out. Julie is having some problems, and we've rushed through to the hospital. The baby's heartbeat is irregular, and they've decided to admit her. Once I'm done here, I need to get back to the shop. I have a couple of urgent orders I need to get out."

"I completely understand! I will let Anaya know. Don't worry about a thing other than helping Julie. Call if you need any additional hands at the shop as well. I can always stop there once I'm done for the day at the church."

Kase relayed the message from his phone call with his brother to Anaya. Both Anaya and Kase were concerned for Julie and the baby at this stage. She hadn't told him how she felt about having children.

Since meeting Julie and his nephews and seeing how ecstatically happy Sam and Julie were as a family, Kase knew that it was something that he wanted. The only difference was that he knew that there was only one person he would ever even imagine having children with. Kase suddenly had a flash of inspiration.

"Hey, Anaya, I'm just stepping out for a couple of minutes. I'll be right back, though, so don't you go anywhere," Kase said in a teasing manner.

"Don't worry, Kase, I know that look of yours. You're up to something! I will wait for you right here."

Kase decided to surprise Anaya with pastries and coffee from her favorite little pastry shop, just around Main Street. This was such a tender moment for Anaya because Kase remembered even the tiniest details about their relationship all those years ago. In the brown paper bag, she found her favorite pastries and coffee exactly as she liked them.

"Some things never change. At times, I could even feel your smile when I was thinking about you so much," he said.

"You thought about me?" Anaya asked.

"Always, Anaya. I would have thought that you would have realized this by now. Are you currently seeing anyone?"

"Kase, it has been so hard for me to try and even get close to anyone else after you left."

Well, aren't you proving to be the asshole by trying to date as many women as you could in an attempt to try and forget about the love of your life, who happens to be standing a couple of feet away from you? Even though you have never gotten serious with anyone, you were still trying to forget about her.

"What about you, Kase?"

He was expecting the question at some point, and now seemed as good a time as any for him to come completely clean with her. He possibly looked like a deer caught in the head-lights for a few moments before he answered her. He was inde-cisive about whether to just be open and honest with her or spin her the same tale. Fortunately for him, he decided to go with the truth. That was another characteristic of their rela-tionship—they could never lie to each other.

"When you didn't show that night, I was so hurt and confused. I'll be honest with you. I saw it as a message that was loud and clear: you no longer wanted me in your life. You have to know that you are and always have been the love of my life, though. So, what I'm going to say now may upset you—or sound cheesy. I've dated a lot of women over the last ten years. The reality is that I was only doing it to try to forget about you, but not even being with these women could help me do that. For most of them, we just went on a single date, and that was enough for me to be able to move on. I've never been able to commit to anyone on a solid relationship level." Kase knew that telling the truth about all of these other women would more than likely hurt Anaya, which really wasn't his intention at all. "You've got to believe me when I say that I've never stopped loving you, Anaya!"

Kase could tell that Anaya's head was working overtime with all the information he'd just offloaded on her. There was no way that he was going to lie to her. Everything was now out in the open, and she had a lot to think about. She decided to focus on the work that needed to be done right now—enough small talk for one day. In what had now become an awkward silence, they started painting. Kase was silently kicking himself for telling her everything. However, he knew he would deal with this rather than face her further down the line if she ever discovered the truth from someone else.

Facing the truth had been a bitter pill for both of them to swallow, but it was the right thing to do. Anaya was definitely feeling betrayed, while Kase felt sad for Anaya that she had chosen to isolate herself from relationships and society because of him.

CHAPTER 10
Never Forgotten

ANAYA WAS STILL TRYING to digest exactly what Kase had been trying to tell her. Despite all the other women he'd dated over the last decade, he was still choosing her. She found her heart racing and was totally shocked when Kase admitted to her that he'd often thought about her. Kase was actually just as single as she was. Maybe there was still hope for them to reconnect. Hope for her to have her happy ending. Perhaps he would change his mind and decide to stay in Elmhurst.

There were so many things racing through her head at the moment that she didn't even want to think about. She and Kase had been apart for so long, and she knew that he was the only man that she really loved. She had always known that, even from their first kiss at the café. She was young and naïve. He was still young and awkward, but what they had decided to build a foundation on was true love. They had always been viewed as one of Elmhurst's young, up-and-coming power couples.

They were each other's backbone, no matter what. They literally stuck up for each other, even when the other person was in the wrong. Their love knew no boundaries, so when Kase just left, the whole town was abuzz with rumors as to what had gone wrong between the two of them. People, typically being nosy, all wanted to be sure that they always knew what was happening with the town gossip. Sam was the first to discover precisely why Anaya had decided not to leave with his brother.

Over the last decade, he had been tempted on many occasions to get a hold of Kase to explain what the situation was regarding Susan's health. Then he remembered just how much Kase hated others interfering in his personal life. Kase had also never asked about her, and Sam felt it wasn't his place to convince Kase to come back to Elmhurst, even if it was to speak with her.

Of course, this was like having a double-edged sword for Sam. He knew that Kase would be furious if he ever found out he knew what was going on and didn't tell Kase about it. Sam knew that his brother was hurting over their relationship. This was one reason for getting Kase and Anaya alone together, allowing them to reconnect. Sam still couldn't tell whether this would be a good idea or just add further fuel to the fire that was already blazing.

After their chat the previous afternoon by the lake, Anaya was hopeful that the two of them would be able to rekindle what used to be a beautiful relationship. She could not bring herself to accept the fact that he had to leave at the end of the month. They had just found each other once more. She had the whole summer holidays ahead of her. What would she do without him? She didn't want to think so much about it. She'd lost so much time away from the man she loved. Was this a second chance for them to get back together?

As they painted next to each other, she splashed a brush of paint on his arm just to get his attention. This was exactly the way they used to laugh and tease each other when they were teenagers. She was hoping to at least get some sort of response from Kase—something that would break the tension between them.

"Oops, sorry!"

"Oh, yeah?" he splashed paint on her arm in retaliation. She started giggling like she used to when they were in high school. Within a matter of minutes, they were both running around the small nursery room, splashing paint at each other. As they began chasing each other, they were soon splashing paint on their arms, their faces, and anywhere else that happened to be in the firing line at the time.

Their childlike natures had come out, and they spent the next ten minutes splashing paint at each other, not really paying attention to what they looked like. Thank goodness there was a solid tarp on the carpet so that the paint didn't destroy any of their hard work so far.

Kase chased after her until he managed to catch up with her. Once again, he wrapped his arms around her and drew her close to him in a firm embrace. She felt safe and secure in the comfort of Kase's muscular arms. Pulling her closer to him once again, they shared another tender kiss.

"I have really missed being able to hold you in my arms like this and kiss you whenever I wanted to. I know that what I said about wanting to forget about you must have hurt you. I'm sorry if it did. I wanted to be honest with you. Do you think that you could ever forgive me?"

"There's really nothing to forgive, Kase. I was the one who stood you up, and I was the one who didn't let you know why, because I thought I was allowing you to follow your dream. I was stupid because I didn't think about how losing our relationship could affect you. I'm sorry that you've gone through the last ten years looking for another me."

"There's only one of you, though, Anaya. I can say that to you honestly because I've met loads of women. None of them make me feel like you do. I don't know if it's because of our history or whether it's because we've been together for such a long time that we're just comfortable with what we know. I'm so confused at the moment."

"This is comfortable. This, with you, feels like home to me, but you know that everything I have right now is here—my home, my teaching career, my parents. I don't know if this small-town girl will ever be able to fit into a big city mentality."

This was what each of them was missing in their lives—the raw spontaneity that comes with true love. It was all becoming very real for both of them, and they weren't sure what they wanted to do with what they were feeling for each other.

CHAPTER 11
Lover's Lane

IT WAS time for the annual Elmhurst Summer Festival. Kase and Anaya decided to go to the festival together again, just like in the old days. When they were younger, they were virtually inseparable, and wherever one was, the other was, too. This year's festival was bigger and better than ever before; it was filled with loads of activities and expected rides that you would find at a fairground attraction.

"Can we go on the rollercoaster together? Remember what happened the last time you were almost threw up? That was so funny! Come on, Kase, let's do it." Anaya was like a young girl on Christmas morning. She wanted to take in as much as she could and do as much as she could with Kase as long as he was in Elmhurst.

This was definitely the very best prescription that Ethan Stone could have ever recommended. Kase couldn't recall being this relaxed in ages.

"Come on, let's go." Anaya dragged Kase by the arm from one side to the next, participating in various other carnival games. It seemed like the past had naturally disappeared, and they were fresh out of high school.

During all their reminiscing, Kase happened to mention their spot out by the lake.

"Remember when we used to go skinny dipping there on all those hot summer nights?" Kase asked. The red glow on Anaya's cheeks gave her away. Yes, she definitely remembered those nights.

"I dare you to come back to the lake with me, and let's go skinny dipping again tonight, once the festival starts winding down," Kase whispered in her ear. Just the sensation of his breath so close to her made her shiver with anticipation.

"You're on," Anaya replied, trying to cover a sudden surge of blushing cheeks.

The rest of the summer festival was fun with its typical trophies and recognition for winning specific games. Kase won Anaya a teddy bear that she promised to love and cherish forever. Kase couldn't help wondering whether she was talking about him or the bear.

"It seems to be getting quite enough out here. Do you want to head out to the lake with me, Miss Mason?" Kase said, teasing her.

"Why I most certainly do, Mr. Chapman, I most certainly do." Just the playful way that she said his name caused Kase to feel aroused and desperate for her tender touch that he knew so well from many years in the past. Kase decided to pull the truck to the entrance and open the door for Anaya. He was a gentleman. Maybe it was to make up for what he knew was about to happen at the lake.

They drove down to their favorite spot and parked under the willow tree that had their initials carved in the middle section of the tree. It didn't take Kase very long to undress completely, leaving a trail of clothes between the truck and the lake.

Anaya was taking her time, leaving each item of clothing neatly folded on the seat of the truck. She had been using the truck as a form of shelter. Not that she was feeling prudish of anything, Kase had seen her plenty of times without her clothes on, especially while they were skinny dipping. This was definitely right up there with being almost as risqué as Anaya was prepared to go with Kase, unless he could make his intentions known. There was only so far Anaya was ready to go with him.

She realized that she was being silly. She loved Kase for who he was. Although it may not have shown by her choice to stay behind, they were both willing to let the past remain in the past for the sake of her sanity, as well as the sanity of those around her.

Anaya ran and dove into the water to catch up to Kase. The lake was refreshingly cool. She placed her arms around his neck, just as she used to do. It was as though they were experiencing things for the first time all over again. Kase circled her tiny waist with one of his arms, using the other to gently caress her face. Her wet hair glistened in the moonlight. It seemed as though everything he ever cared about had brought him right back to this moment.

Anaya pulled his head down to hers, allowing him to devour her as he had flashbacks of them making out in this very spot in the past. Anaya had been a virgin and had allowed Kase to tenderly deflower her. She had enjoyed the intimacy of being with him. It felt natural and comfortable. Kase had not forced himself on her. Instead, he allowed things to progress naturally, exploring every inch of her body by the light of the moon.

She could feel him becoming aroused. Her own hunger for intimate passion with the man that she loved was causing her to feel a searing heat running throughout her body. Her nipples were hard, inviting Kase to explore them even further with his tongue, which he did, letting out some gentle moans as he did so.

"Oh, Anaya, you have no idea how much I have missed this. How much I have missed your perfect body and the way you feel whenever we're together. I don't know if I'm going to be able to control myself much more around you tonight! I have to have you!" Kase whispered in her ear.

This set Anaya off even further. She took one of Kase's hands and directed him between her legs. Whispering in his ear, she said, "Can you feel what you're doing to me? I need you inside me. I need you now!" She was almost whimpering, and Kase knew that they were both driving each other almost over the edge.

"I must warn you, I haven't slept with anyone since you, so please don't expect this to be long-lasting! The other thing is that I don't have a condom, Anaya. I don't know how safe it is to do this." His protests were met with more groans from Anaya.

"Forget about the condom. I am on contraceptives. We are safe! Kase, I really need you now!" She begged him to allow her to mount his rock-hard cock, which made Kase groan.

Together, they found their rhythm, and it didn't take long before they both climaxed simultaneously. Anaya couldn't believe just how much she had missed making love to Kase. She thought about all their long, passionate lovemaking at their spot on the other side of the waterfall. Kase faced down toward her voluptuous, full breasts, which were now standing completely upright. Had this really happened?

They were still in a content embrace.

Kase kissed her on the top of her head and whispered in her ear, "I still love you so much, Anaya!"

"I love you too, Kase; I'm sorry it's taken me a long time to realize just how much!"

Neither of them was paying any attention to what was

happening around them to notice the car headlights getting closer.

"KASE CHAPMAN!" The sound of silence around the lake was suddenly broken by Joe Mason's booming voice.

How did he actually even find them, and how long had he been there? Had he actually watched their whole lovemaking? What was making him so angry?

Anaya was shocked to the point that, even under the moonlight, Kase could see the color drain from her face. She knew exactly what the tone in her father's voice meant and wasn't about to have a full-on run-in with him, especially not after the tender experience she had just had with Kase.

Embarrassed to be caught out by her father, Anaya immediately pulled away from Kase.

"When are you going to start behaving like a grown man instead of constantly playing around with my daughter's good name and her reputation?"

With that, Anaya slunk out of the lake, making her way back to Kase's truck and quickly putting her clothes back on. She was still embarrassed by having to face her father and his wrath.

"Anaya has a reputation to uphold as a schoolteacher in this town. You are skating on very thin ice. Her reputation could easily be ruined by all of your shenanigans here tonight."

Kase decided that it was time for him to stand up for both him and Anaya and take on Joe.

"With all due respect, pastor, Anaya is an adult. Surely she's old enough to be making these kinds of decisions on her own. I honestly don't feel like I owe you any explanation."

"I'm so sorry for behaving so recklessly, Dad." Anaya said, doing a complete turnaround.

Kase felt like a complete idiot, having taken Joe Mason on in front of Anaya. He would never have believed that Anaya would take her father's side of this argument. He felt like maybe he'd been a jerk here, and Anaya actually enjoyed being coddled by her parents.

Kase drove Anaya home, and there was total silence all the way. He was leaving in two weeks. Maybe it was best that they just leave things as they were and not pursue this relationship any further. Kase was very disappointed in the way that Anaya took her father's side. As far as Kase was concerned, the only thing that they may have done wrong was to make love in such a public place.

CHAPTER 12
Kase, Come Back

WHEN KASE DIDN'T SHOW up to help at the church the next day, Anaya felt a mix of guilt and remorse. She hated to admit it, but she was missing his company already. *Oh boy, if this is how I'm feeling already, what will I likely experience when he really leaves?* She thought to herself.

Not wanting to think about it any further, she continued stacking all the children's books and some of the toys on the newly constructed bookshelves. Joe stopped by to see how the work was progressing. He was so impressed by the complete transformation that had taken place over just a few days. He complimented her on a job well done and commented on the vast improvement between what it looked like previously and what it looked like now. Anaya credited Kase for all of his hard work and told her dad that they really made a great team.

"My child, you can do so much better than chasing after some punk who has nothing better to do with his life than gamble. There are still all those other gentlemen from the church that I've had lined up for you for ages now. Every single one of them has excellent reputations in town."

"You know what, Dad? I resent your comments about Kase. He's always been respectful toward you. He's probably one of the hardest-working people you'll ever come across. Why don't you like him? What has Kase Chapman ever done to you?"

"I do like him. I just don't think that he's good enough for you. You have much better options available to you than the likes of him, sweetheart!"

"You do realize that I'm actually a grown woman now, and I don't really need your approval or permission to see whoever I want to see. You have always been so overprotective of me, even when I was much younger. Whenever something went wrong, you would jump in and save the day like it was your responsibility! I know that you may think you were doing me a favor, but in the meantime, you were actually tying my hands behind my back and not allowing me to go out there and try new things. You've made me feel like I need your approval for everything."

No sooner had she finished with her rant at her father than Anaya had a moment of clarity, maybe for the first time ever. She realized that her decision to stick by her father's side the previous night after the incident at the lake had probably hurt Kase, the one person she never wanted to hurt again. By responding to her father the way she had, she was basically hanging Kase out to dry, which was the last thing she ever wanted to do. Her dad was actually in the wrong by stalking them at the summer festival and spying on them.

Doing her best not to think of the few days that Kase had left in town, she headed home. Climbing into the shower to cool off, she washed her worries of the day away. Dressing in a cool summer top with a pair of shorts and sandals, Anaya decided that it was time to go shopping for candy. Her main intention was to sneak into Kase's parents' home that night to speak with him. No doubt he would be staying in his old childhood bedroom, which Anaya knew only too well.

CHAPTER 13
Time to Catch Up

THE SUMMER BREEZE blowing through the trees was still too hot and uncomfortable. Kase tossed and turned as he was trying to sleep. He tried harder not to think about Anaya and the loneliness he felt. He realized that he needed to use the rest of the time in Elmhurst to actually heal. Curiosity over what was happening with his casinos was getting the better of him, and he went to the kitchen, returning with his mom's iPad.

He had been wondering for a while now about what was happening with his company. He thought about the managers he'd placed in charge of each casino in his absence, as well as the top most senior manager who helped him oversee all business transactions. He needed to be sure he wasn't walking back into a hornet's nest. Most would be completely under control without a doubt, but he needed to know if he was losing the Silver Palms Salt Lake Casino or not.

Three taps on his window caught him completely off guard, causing such a knee-jerk reaction that he almost dropped the iPad. Immediately, Kase's heart started racing, and he smiled. Only one person knew their secret tap code, which had been formed years ago. It had to be Anaya. She was the only person who knew the three-tap code. She'd done it so many times before that Kase could instantly recognize the pattern of her code, even after ten years. Three was their secret number.

Opening the blinds only to be met by her sheepish grin under the lights took Kase back down memory lane. He helped her through the window.

"I'm so sorry I didn't stand up for you when my dad approached us."

"I forgive you if you've shown up with all the candy!" She dumped the bag of various chocolate candies on his bed. They'd done this before as teenagers, eating different flavors to assess which ones were the best.

The candy ritual was usually a way for them to make up or if something had happened that made the other crazy. Kase was actually surprised that Anaya still remembered what seemed like a silly tradition. She had bought most of his favorite candies to make up for the situation with her father.

"I straightened things out with my dad," she told Kase. She wanted him to feel that he could trust her with anything. If their relationship was going to go anywhere, this single situation needed to be put in the past and left there.

"You really didn't need to do that on my account."

"Kase, I never did it for you. I did it for me. After the other night, I realized just how much my father has been holding me back and how he's prevented me from moving forward with the life that I really want. He's constantly trying to match me with men from the church that are really not my type. I'm getting sick of it right now."

"So, what is your type?" Kase teased her by pulling her against his chest.

"Hmmm... Let me think about that for a while?" she teased him right back.

They shared an intimate kiss. Anaya tasted exactly like the chocolates they'd just been eating.

"You taste like chocolate mint, one of my favorites!" he told her.

"What am I going to do when you leave Elmhurst?" She started looking serious. "Kase, we have only just found one another. I don't want to lose what we have." Once again, there seemed to be a sense of sadness lurking behind her big brown eyes.

"What are you hiding from me, Anaya? Your eyes are so sad. There are some things that you aren't telling me." Kase asked her sincerely.

"I think that you know how I feel about you and about us... I don't know if I will survive if you leave again. I know that you believed that I made a choice willingly the last time you left. The truth is that it almost ate me up inside. I don't know if I will be able to go through this same experience all over again." Anaya was beginning to look even more sensitive and sad.

"What are you thinking?" Kase had always been able to read Anaya like a book, but not this time. Her sadness seems to be deep-rooted.

"I'm just so happy to have you back in my life, but the thought of you leaving again is going to tear me up all over again. I hope you realize that it's always been you and nobody but you!"

"I feel exactly the same way. You may think that I have dated a lot of women looking to move on. The truth is that with each of those women, I was looking for something of you in each of them, or in one of them at least. Do you know that there wasn't one single one of them that could ever hold a candle to you?"

"Have a miniature Hershey bar. Do you remember how many times we've actually done this? Anaya asked.

"Way too many times for me to remember. I've got to admit, though, that it's so much better now."

"That's because these are "make up" chocolates!" she joked.

"But isn't that always the best kind?"

"Tell me more about the life of Kase Chapman away from Elmhurst."

"There's not all that much to tell, really. You know that I'm not married or even attached. I'm responsible for the eight casinos dotted all over between the west coast and the east coast. I manage a total staff complement of about fifty thousand people, depending on whether it's the season or not. Because I spend most of my time in Vegas, I live in a penthouse suite that's been converted into an apartment on the top floor at the Silver Palms Vegas hotel. Two years ago, I bought a holiday home for myself in San Diego. It's a beautiful villa, but I very seldom get to go there because of my crazy work schedule. What more do you want to know? What about you? Try and sum your life up for me in a couple of sentences."

"Well, you already know the reason why I stood you up the night we were supposed to run away together. I still feel really awful about that, but there was no way I could leave my mom to go through what she went through on her own. It took about five to six years to just get her treatments under control, where my dad could also take over from me for a bit instead of relying completely on me. That's one of the reasons I took on teaching. It gave me enough freedom to still take care of my mom and earn enough money to support myself in the process. I'm not going to say that it's been easy, but mom has been cancer-free for the last two years, even though it took a lot out of her."

"What did you—or do you—really want to be doing with your life, though? If you could have anything in the world, right now, what would it be?"

"Money will always be something we can't live without; however, it doesn't really drive me all that much to the point where I'd say that I really need an excessive amount to live off of. If I really have to think about it, one of the things I would really do anything to have right now would be a family of my own." Kase could see the loneliness in her eyes, and now he understood why. She spent her days surrounded by children. Because she was not married or even dating anyone, her prospects of having children were becoming slimmer and slimmer as each day passed.

He felt like a total jerk for even imagining that Anaya had moved on with children. He also realized that he needed to do everything he possibly could to get her to Vegas to see the quality of life that he led. Nobody at home even knew what Kase was worth financially. All that they knew was that he managed casinos.

The sun was starting to rise, and Kase realized that, once again, just as they had done many, many times before, they had spent the whole night talking to each other about things that were important to them.

CHAPTER 14
Guess Who's Coming

A LATER THAT SAME MORNING, Anaya stopped by her parent's home on her way to meet up with Kase at the church. She was there to speak with her mom.

"Mom, you know that the last thing I'd ever want to do is give you some added pressure while you're still trying to overcome this cancer that's taken over almost the last decade of your life..." Anaya's voice was beginning to betray her.

"Anaya, you should know that whatever you tell me here and now sticks between us. If you want this conversation to be totally confidential, then that's exactly what it will be. I need you to trust me, so you know you can talk about absolutely everything and anything. My darling child, what's on your mind right now?"

"Oh, Mom, you don't know how it feels to suddenly have the love of your life back in your life, where you possibly get another chance with them. I'm so confused at the moment when it comes to what to do. I don't know if I should just risk it all and get away with Kase to see how it goes or whether to call it quits right here and right now so that it was a nice summer romance."

Diana could see the tears in her daughter's eyes, and she felt her pain.

"Anaya, I'm not going to pretend to even know what's going through your mind at the moment. I'm so sorry you are hurting so badly. I wish that I could just take all the pain away and just leave you with all the happy memories. I can see the way the two of you look at each other, though, and there's definitely an undeniable spark between you. I can't make the decision for you, but I can tell you what I would do if I was in your situation."

"Please, Mom? Any sound advice would do right now. I haven't been able to discuss this with anyone, and it's eating me up inside. I literally feel ill whenever I think that I may need to make a major life-changing decision here. One of my other obstacles is everything that I have here. I have my job. I love the children that I teach. I have you and dad, who I can just stop past at any given moment, and I know you are always here for me. I'm so torn between being loyal to Elmhurst that I honestly don't know what I want to do other than be closer to Kase."

"Well, there you have it, Anaya; you have actually made your decision already—or at least subconsciously. The heart will always go after exactly what it wants. You have been fortunate to have found each other again after all these years. It's serendipity that neither of you is already married, but I think that speaks more to the fact that you had always hoped he'd come back to Elmhurst. Now that he's here, what are you waiting for?

"What do I do, Mom? I know he needs to go back to Vegas sometime really soon, and I am dreading it. It's going to be like losing him ten years ago all over again. Your dad is always so condescending toward Kase! I have no idea why he feels this way other than because of a few mischievous harmless pranks. He was still a child! What happened to forgiveness? Is he going to be forced to carry that label around with him forever, seeing as dad disapproves of him so much?"

"Now, now, my child, don't you fret about your father. I will deal with him, and he will be on his very best behavior. Why don't you invite Kase over for dinner this evening? It seems only fitting to thank him for all his hard work alongside you in the nursery. I love this boy myself, my girl. He has a whole lot of spunk and isn't scared of hard work. You could definitely be doing yourself a great disservice if you didn't at least try to listen to what's going on in his head right now," Diana said.

"But dad is always so rude and condescending toward Kase. I honestly don't know how Kase has been able to keep a tight control over his temper when it comes to dealing with Daddy and his snide remarks."

"I will make sure that he's on his best behavior."

Diana shared how she met Joe and how he wasn't such a perfect individual. Everyone had made him out to be the pastor of the local congregation.

"As much as your father is totally against you and Kase being together, I can see what's going on between the two of you. You've been given a second chance at this. This allows you to get the love of your life back permanently, Anaya! You can't let this chance slip by you again."

"Why don't you invite him to dinner? Maybe your dad will slowly warm to the idea. I know he will accept him. Still, he's probably worried that you will leave town and follow Kase wherever his business ventures are."

"I hear what you are saying, Mom, but haven't women been doing that same thing for hundreds of years? Following the men in their lives to new frontiers? I need to be sure that wherever I'm following Kase, it's actually to the right destination. The last thing I need right now is to follow him and then nothing comes of it, or worse, I end up hating the lifestyle."

"Yes, my girl, but how will you know any of these things unless you are actually prepared to use your gut instinct as your guide? To go and see whether there is something there? If not, you always have a home that you can come back to in Elmhurst."

A few hours later, Anaya and Kase finally finish painting the nursery. Stepping back to admire their handiwork, Anaya dropped a first-class challenge for Kase.

"So, how do you feel about joining my family and me for dinner this evening?"

"Do I really have a choice? Is this some kind of set-up by your father?"

"No, it was mom's idea!"

"In that case, count me in." Kase had all the time in the world for Diana, which was part of the reason he was so upset that nobody had informed him that she had been very sick for so long.

His pure spontaneity was one of the qualities Anaya really admired about him. He knew that he'd be walking directly into the lion's den when it came to Joe Mason, but he weighed up the odds. If he wanted to try and win them over and receive her parents' blessing to at least be able to take her away for a couple of days before he had to officially resume his duties in Vegas or wherever else there happened to be some crisis that needed to be managed, he was going to go for broke this evening at dinner.

Kase had no sooner arrived at the Masons' home than the pastor began what felt like the Spanish Inquisition:

"So, Kase, what are your plans for the immediate future?"

"I definitely have to go back because I need to find out what is happening with each of my businesses across the US. Unfortunately, I can't leave the work unattended in the casino industry. There's too much that can go wrong too quickly. I have to be able to manage my work hands-on." Kase stopped for a second or two and, looking at Anaya, added, "I'm really hoping that Anaya will come back for a week's holiday with me, though." He squeezed Anaya's hand.

This was Joe's master plan all along. Kase would reveal his true intentions to uproot Anaya. All he wanted was for Kase to leave Anaya behind. He thought that Anaya would rather battle things on her own in Elmhurst for the rest of her life than be totally happy with a plan to leave.

Kase had called it as he saw it much earlier. They were just two different, independent people. She really wanted to be around her parents, whatever life she believed she had in Elmhurst, her comfy home, and her students. For Anaya to be okay with leaving, it was going to take a miracle. Nonetheless, it was one that Kase was willing to gamble on.

Throughout dinner, the conversation seemed to have taken on a much more subdued tone. While Anaya was not too fond of leaving, she tried not to dwell on it too much. She didn't want her father to continue drilling Kase with questions that were not only uncomfortable for her but especially uncomfortable for Kase. Besides, a week's holiday in the big city may be just what she needed right now, especially away from the prying eyes of people in the community.

The following Sunday, Kase went to church with Anaya. During his sermon, Joe expressed gratitude to Kase, Sam, Anaya, and the rest of the ladies for their hard work in renovating the church's nursery as well as for creating an entirely new flower bed at the entrance to the church.

CHAPTER 15
Taking a Chance

"ANAYA, we basically have a week before I return to Vegas and the madness starts all over again. I would really like to spend this time with you and only you. I don't want to share you with Elmhurst and have your father stalk us at every turn. Please think about coming back with me a week earlier. We can spend the time together really getting to know each other now that we're adults." Kase had made a passionate plea, hoping she would say yes. "I want you to know, though, that I'm not going to push you into anything that you're not comfortable with. I love you way too much to do that to you. If you're happier here, then I will respect that."

Kase was now the one who looked pained, and Anaya hated to see him like this. It was one of the first glimpses she got of him when he and Sam first showed up on her doorstep three weeks prior.

"You can come on an open-ended ticket, Anaya. If you're not happy and you want to come back to Elmhurst, it can be arranged for you right away. The last thing I want this week to be for you is challenging. I want us to be able to get to know each other properly again. We've been busy here ever since I arrived, and while we've had a whole lot of fun working side by side at the church and at your home, I really want you to catch a glimpse of my world—the world that I want you to share with me."

Kase wasn't mincing his words; he said them exactly as they were, and Anaya respected him for it. This was a side of Kase that she'd never seen before, one where he was taking control of the situation without hesitation.

She'd caught a glimpse of this when her father stalked them at the lake. She realized that Kase was possibly not the pushover that everyone assumed. Sure, he was taking things pretty calmly when he first arrived in Elmhurst—probably because of his heart. This was another side of Kase, one that was confident and made decisions instead of allowing others to walk all over him. Anaya realized that there was still a lot to learn about this man, and maybe a week or so would be the perfect opportunity for this. She was dying to see him in his own environment.

"Sure, let's do this! I'm interested to see what happens over there and what makes that lifestyle work for you. I want to get to know what your life is all about."

With that, Kase made a call to arrange for their flight to San Diego. They were both grateful that she had the whole of the summer off and could spend some quality time with him —some alone time. She wanted to see what he'd been doing with himself for the last ten years.

They were all set to leave the following day. Anaya was trying to get as much information out of Kase as possible about what she needed to pack for this "open-ended vacation."

"Pack whatever you're going to feel comfortable in. Whatever you don't have, we can always go shopping for." Kase planned to spoil Anaya as much as possible on this holiday while still showing her why he was so excited and passionate about life in the casino industry. They were both pleased that he still had at least one week left of recovery time, during which they could spend the days away from Elmhurst.

While Kase loved his parents and family, he had reached the point where he needed his own space again. He needed to be making the decisions. He wanted his life back. Elmhurst had been fun to come back to. He would always be grateful to Ethan Stone for insisting he go somewhere quiet because this had brought him and Anaya back together. It was time to go home now, though.

Elmhurst had been fun. It had given him time to reminisce and bring back some amazing memories of a life gone by, but that's precisely what it was—a life gone by. Kase knew he could never integrate back into a small-town lifestyle, especially not one where he felt that his style was totally cramped. He was beginning to feel claustrophobic, which was one of the parts of his job that he loved. No two days were exactly the same. He had large spaces and territory to cover at any given time. It was the sheer adrenaline pumping through his veins every single day.

Thanking his parents for all that they'd done for him during his recovery time, giving his brother, Julie, and his nephews each a hug goodbye, he promised not to be such a stranger. He believed that one way or another, his connection to Elmhurst was not likely to be severed anytime soon, as long as Anaya insisted on staying there.

He made one more stop before heading toward Arcata Airport. Anaya's home.

She had two small cases already packed and looked gorgeous as ever in a floral summer dress. It came above her knees, giving everyone full appreciation for her long legs. She was wearing sandals with a slight heel.

"You are looking gorgeous as always! Ready for this adventure, Anaya?"

"I'm super excited. Come on, Kase, let's go already! I'm dying to see what all the fuss is about in your world." Anaya was dead serious, and Kase liked her openness to discovering his world.

Meanwhile, little did Anaya know she was about to experience the other side of Kase Chapman—the casino industry side, that full-blown power leadership with a no-nonsense approach. Something about Kase that she'd never witnessed before.

By 9:00 a.m., they managed to leave Anaya's home. For Kase, this was exactly how things should have played out ten years ago, with the girl, his truck, and the promise of a brand-new future ahead of them. The only difference now was that Anaya wouldn't have to witness all the struggles that he'd gone through over the last ten years. She got to see the results.

Arriving at the Arcata Airport, Kase handed the keys back to the rental agency, and they made their way to the VIP area. There, waiting for them, was the Gulfstream. It was fueled and ready to go. Anaya's eyes were wide opened, showing both astonishment and amazement.

"How can you afford any of this, Kase?" she asked.

"It just so happens that I know the owner of a couple of casinos!" he answered her with a cheeky grin on his face.

There was a high level of luxury on the private jet, complete with staff to see to their every need. Once the Gulfstream was airborne, they were offered drinks. Kase asked for his usual. Anaya began to see a completely different side of Kase. Kase was in a completely different space in this environment. Here, he was comfortable and confident. Everything about sitting in this luxurious environment seemed to suit him perfectly.

Anaya settled on a martini while they brought Kase an amber liquid with lots of ice. He'd occasionally had brandy years ago when they were still young and reckless, but he'd always had a mixer with it. Her martini arrived, and it was clear that she was excited for this time with Kase.

"Here's to whatever the next week or so may hold in store for us. Thank you for deciding to take a chance on me, Anaya! I love you. Cheers!"

The flight had about three and a half hours to move into a holding pattern, and it was confirmed that they were about to land in San Diego. Anaya was about to see what Kase's holiday home looked like—the one he'd bought himself as a thirtieth birthday present.

A driver was waiting for them as they disembarked from the jet. She still had no idea that Kase was worth billions. Anyone meeting him for the first time would immediately pick up that he was an extremely hard worker who had a solid work ethic and moral code of standards that he not only chose to live and work by but also expected the same from each of his staff.

This didn't always go down so well in the casino industry because there was usually a lot of side hustling. This was something that Kase refused to tolerate at any of his resorts. You were either loyal to Kase and the casino without question, or you were out on your ass! There were no in-betweens with Kase. He was very much a down-to-earth, straight-shooting, black-and-white businessman. He was extremely professional and successful at everything he did. For many in the hotel and gaming industry, Kase was well-respected and marked as a serious contender not to be messed with.

The drive didn't take them all that long from the airport, and they were soon pulling up the driveway at a beautiful double-story villa just off Buccaneer Way. Anaya was shocked by the sheer size and beauty of the property. They were greeted by Sarita, the housekeeper. She had arranged for Paulo, one of the staff, to transfer their bags from the trunk to the main bedroom. The first thing that Anaya did was explore the villa.

This was something that had always fascinated Kase about Anaya. There were times when she was so innocent in her childlike wonder, even at thirty. She could make something as simple as coming into a new environment an adventure!

Anaya couldn't believe that Kase had such excellent taste when it came to the furnishings and décor of his private home. She was shocked by the sheer luxury of his home. Each of the oversized bedrooms within the house had its own private bathroom and walk-in closet. The main bedroom was about four times the size of her main bedroom at home.

The room featured a king-size extra-long bed, which looked incredibly inviting. Each of the paintings on the wall blended with all the elements in the room. Knowing a little about art, Anaya knew that these were originals rather than prints. Kase would have either had to have them specially commissioned for him or buy them at auction for a pretty penny.

Along the entire length of one of the bedroom walls were glass stack doors that opened onto a large deck. On one side of the deck was a luxurious hot tub, and on the other side were wicker loungers with padded seats and oversized cushions. Directly below the deck was an infinity pool where the water was retrieved and pumped back into the pool with jets.

Everything looked so comfortable and inviting. Although the house was huge, she could see Kase's personal touch throughout. It was clearly a man's home that needed a feminine touch to round it off completely. Only a woman would be able to tell what was lacking. Mentally, she already imagined what she would change or move around if she and Kase were to make this permanent.

Can you hear how ridiculous you're sounding? Are you really prepared to give up your comfortable life in Elmhurst for this? What makes you think you will actually be able to handle the fast-paced life of the casino industry?

"What do you want to do first?" Kase was suddenly behind her with his arms wrapped around her waist. "Oooh, this is a feeling that I never want to forget or lose sight of again. I've lost you once before. What do I have to do to keep you with me?" His voice sounded sincere and husky. Anaya could tell that he was really turned on at the moment.

"It's been a long, hot day so far. Maybe we can cool down in the pool?" Anaya placed emphasis on "cool down". She felt that Kase may be trying to move things along a little bit quicker than she'd prepared to go right now. Instead, she would take things one day at a time and get to know him again before being totally willing to commit. Anaya knew that this time, when she actually committed, it would be forever rather than just a summer stopover.

"I need you to give me the time that I need, Kase. I don't want this to just be a summer romance. If we're in this thing together, then you've got to know that I'm all in. It's going to take the same sort of commitment from you as well. I just want to take it a bit slower."

"Sure, Anaya, whatever is going to make you happy." Kase wouldn't push her too hard. "I lost you once, though, but you need to know that I'm not likely to give you up so willingly this time! Let's head out to the pool."

The pool deck was directly below the balcony for the main bedroom, and Kase headed downstairs. He had swimming trunks in one of the guests changing areas downstairs, just off of the deck. While there, he asked Sarita to make them some Sangria.

After her last comments, he still wasn't entirely sure where he stood with Anaya, but if she needed her space, he was prepared to give that to her until she could figure things out on her own. Kase dove in and swam several laps before Anaya joined him in the pool. She tied her hair in a high ponytail, and Kase just burst out laughing.

"What's so funny?" Anaya asked.

"Anaya, the last time you wore your hair like that, and we were in the water together... well, you know exactly how it ended! Now you want to come and tease me with that same look again? You tell me that you want to take things slow, but then you come out here wearing that sexy little bikini, looking exactly like you did in your senior year! How am I supposed to take you seriously or control myself around you?" Kase was half-pleading with her.

Thankfully, Sarita arrived with a massive pitcher of Sangria that had all sorts of berries in it along with loads of crushed ice.

"Welcome to my home in San Diego, Anaya." Kase was embarrassed, but he reverted back to his charm. Pouring her a glass as well as one for himself, he made a toast to her health and happiness. "Seeing as you are going to make this trip as challenging for me as possible because you're not making it easy for me, I think we need to take a drive through to the casino this evening and see if there's a show that you're interested in seeing."

"I don't know if I have anything suitable for me to wear to any of these shows in the casino," she confessed to Kase while they were enjoying their drinks as the warm San Diego sun glistened off the water.

"Don't worry about anything—we'll get that sorted out in no time for you. Give me a few minutes." He hopped out of the pool with his sandy hair wet and disheveled. He quickly made a phone call and dove back in the pool to cool off once more.

After soaking up some afternoon sun, they headed inside to get ready for the evening. Walking back into the master bedroom, Anaya found an array of outfits for her to choose from to wear to the casino. There were shoes, bags, and even some sexy lingerie. They were all the right size as well.

"How did you manage to get all of this right?" She was completely astonished.

"I told you that whatever you didn't have, we would go shopping for it. It just so happens that I have a personal shopper in San Diego. That was who I phoned earlier."

Anaya was totally blown away. Who was this man, and what had he done with Kase?

Arriving at the San Diego casino, everyone greeted them from the moment they walked in. Kase reminded them that he was still officially on leave for a week and that they needed to carry on as if he was not even there. He asked that they be treated as any regular couple in the hotel.

Naturally, however, the service was VIP all the way. Kase treated Anaya to several different cabaret acts and musical performances that were taking place in the various theaters in the casino.

Anaya was so in love with the home in San Diego. Their time there had been blissful. She'd spent time in the pool every day, managed to work on her tan, and she and Kase had been enjoying some serious time catching up with each other during the day.

At night, they went out for dinner at some of the finest dining establishments in San Diego, followed by cocktails in the hot tub back at the house. They were able to just be themselves without having to worry about Joe Mason jumping out of the bushes and reprimanding them for making love to each other.

For the first time, Anaya felt that she would be able to live with this man no matter where he was. The way he made love to her was always gentle, unless they both got totally carried away in the heat of the moment.

He and Anaya could have the run of the entire mansion without prying eyes. They had a natural affinity for water; probably because that was the first time they had ever made love in their secret lake in Elmhurst. Kase discovered that taking Anaya in water turned her on. Whether it was the infinity pool, the hot tub, or even the shower, there was something that made her exceptionally moist and inviting.

Kase would often start their encounter outside and end up carrying her to his king-sized, bed where he could take his time over every inch of her body. His tongue would tease each of her perky nipples as he held each one in his hands, sending her just to the edge of ecstasy and then letting her come back down to earth again.

He enjoyed watching her writhe and squirm as he devoured her, with his tongue gently teasing her. Anaya would arch her back, clutching the satin sheets and biting down on her bottom lip as she became more and more aroused by Kase.

He knew exactly what to do to her and with her for them to finally be able to reach the point of no return.

After several hot and heavy sessions, they would lie in each other's arms. Anaya would snuggle under Kase's arm, totally content. Anaya seemed like she couldn't be happier with her life.

CHAPTER 16
An Unburied Past

BY THE FIFTH night in San Diego, Kase mentioned that they needed to fly to Vegas. He needed to get some stuff sorted out. Moreover, he wanted to show Anaya the penthouse that he'd been living in for several years already. Anaya said she was looking forward to seeing him in his own natural habitat—the hotels where he was most often, between the Silver Palms Vegas and Silver Sands Vegas.

By the time the Gulfstream landed in Vegas, there was a car waiting for them. The driver greeted Kase. He was one of the hotel's full-time employees who drove Kase around whenever he was in town. Kase was pretty excited to show Anaya the massive penthouse. He'd called ahead to arrange for it to be cleaned from top to bottom, so no surprises were waiting for Anaya. He didn't want her to get the wrong impression of his life as a bachelor.

His main aim was to show her the time of her life at the Silver Palms Vegas, but first, they'd do a bit of sightseeing in Vegas itself. Kase took her down the Vegas strip, past most of the famous tourist attractions. He knew that it was probably kind of cheesy to do so, but with a bit of luck, she'd agreed to his invitation to move out to Vegas to be with him. After all, if she ever felt homesick, he could send her back with the jet whenever she wanted.

Kase had everything planned that he wanted to say to her. He was feeling as nervous as hell in case she shot him down. There should be no reason she would, though; they had just spent almost the perfect week together. He was not satisfied with just a week, though. He wanted Anaya all to himself, just as they had initially agreed ten years ago.

On their first night in Vegas, Kase booked an exclusive booth at one of the most romantic restaurants at the hotel. He ordered the most exquisite bouquet of red roses, her favorite. He arranged for them to be delivered to the penthouse shortly before leaving for the restaurant. All the card read was, "Now and forever yours, J." That night was the night that he needed to convince Anaya to stay with him in Vegas. He wanted the perfect romantic evening so she could get an idea of the life-style that Kase was offering her.

Arriving at the restaurant, he ordered an expensive bottle of champagne. Waiting to propose a toast, he took her hands in his over the table and began to tell her what had been on his mind for the last month.

"Anaya, you know that I can't live without you. I think that you feel the same way about me, or at least I hope you do. Please think very seriously about moving here, where you and I can give this relationship a real shot at working."

As they were deep in their conversation, Vicky was passing by but stopped by their table when she noticed Kase.

"Hey, Kase, I was really beginning to give up on you! Have you been ghosting me since the last time you stood me up? You should know that I don't give up that easily, and now you are seriously going to have to make it all up to me in a big way. I've been calling and texting you for like a month now, and you've been totally ignoring every single message. Was there something wrong with our last date? I really thought it went off extremely well; we're definitely compatible, and you know exactly what it is that I'm after!"

All the while, throughout Vicky's monologue, Kase was trying to get her to shut up and just go away. He didn't even have time to introduce Anaya to her properly or give Anaya the heads-up to let her know who she was. Kase could see the look coming from Anaya, and he realized that he had some serious explaining to do. The moment Vicky took a breath, Kase jumped in and introduced Anaya to her. Unfortunately, he wasn't able to get much more than that in, as long as Vicky carried on talking.

Anaya's blood was already boiling. She was convinced that Kase was lying to her about all the women in his life; here stood one living proof. Why had he been playing her along like this? Anaya was on the verge of tears when she got up from the table and made a beeline for the penthouse suite.

She was not sticking around for a moment longer than necessary. She couldn't blame Kase for being all taken in by the beauty and good looks of all the hotel croupiers. They were literally hired for their good looks and abilities to land the big clients by playing on their deepest desires. If this was what Kase was after in a relationship, then she had really been duped by him. There was no point in staying for even one more day.

Pushing Vicky aside, Kase ran after Anaya and just missed the penthouse elevator. He would now have to wait until it came back down again. Vicky had followed him to the elevator. Kase was now seething because she was being a bimbo and didn't understand that he was just not interested in her.

"Vicky, you know what? I think you need to back off now and leave me alone. You have just caused so much damage for me that you'd better hope I can go back and undo it. If not,

I'm afraid that your days at the Silver Palms Vegas are over. Please don't ever call me again! The woman that you have just chased away from here is the love of my life. Suppose I happen to lose her over something stupid that you've just said. In that case, I swear..." Suddenly the elevator arrived, but Kase had made his speech, and by the looks of things, Vicky had finally gotten the message.

Arriving at his penthouse suite, Kase found Anaya packing her bags.

"Anaya, I promise you that Vicky meant and still means absolutely nothing to me. I've been trying to get her to stop stalking me for ages. She simply won't stop calling and texting me. I have told her to leave me alone on several occasions, but she doesn't listen," he explained.

"Oooh, Kase, you're so full of it! That's not even what I'm mad about. I wasn't expecting you to still be waiting for me... What really got me going tonight is that you couldn't even introduce me as your girlfriend!" Anaya was dead serious and looked extremely hurt. Kase knew her well enough to be able to tell just by looking at her eyes.

"Come on, babe; when was I supposed to introduce you? She never even gave me a moment to get a word in edgeways." Kase was trying to reason with Anaya and get her to stop frantically packing.

"This has been a mistake! I should never have agreed to come to San Diego or Vegas with you. I knew that it was going to end with someone getting hurt. Let's face it, we are just from two completely different worlds, and I definitely don't see myself fitting into this fast-paced one." Anaya was on the verge of tears.

"Anaya, please, you've got to believe me. Nothing is going on between us. We went out for a couple of drinks twice, and now she thinks that we're in a relationship."

"So, you did go out with her! That's exactly my point,

Kase. I know that if I'm here, it's just going to cramp your life-style even further. I'd rather go home to Elmhurst, where I know what's going to happen from one day to the next."

"Yes, where everything is so bland and boring!" Immediately after the words left Kase's mouth, he regretted uttering them. Anaya's voice was now almost shrill, and Kase was grateful that they were actually in the penthouse apartment.

"Bland and boring? Bland and boring? I must remind you, Kase, that 'bland and boring' was your life once upon a time. Don't think that you're so high and mighty now that you're living and working in Vegas.

"I'd like to go home now, please! As in, NOW!" Anaya's words were so adamant and so final that Kase decided to give in and just let her go.

"Let me take you home with the jet, so at least I know that you arrived in Elmhurst safely. I can have it fueled and ready to go within the hour if you really want to go."

"I don't need your fancy jet! I'm quite happy to fly commercial. I really don't want anything from you anymore."

"I'll phone the airport and book you a ticket. Let me at least take you to the airport?"

"No! Kase, I really just think that we need to leave things as they are. If you could arrange the ticket and someone to take me to the airport, I'd be grateful. Other than that, I really don't want anything else from you right now."

"Anaya, please don't go when you're in this state. Can we not just sit down and work things out like we always used to do back in the good old days?" Kase made one last-ditch attempt at reasoning things through with her.

"No, Kase, what's done is done. I simply made a huge mistake by agreeing to come here. I was right all along. I don't belong in a big city. Elmhurst is probably about the right pace for me. I was happy with my life there. Why did you have to come and turn everything upside down again for me?"

"What more do you want me to say? I have apologized now. I don't know how many times, Anaya. Don't you think that you're also a little bit unreasonable? You are holding me to a much higher standard. It's been ten years since we last saw each other. Naturally, certain things would have changed. I'll tell you what hasn't changed as far as I'm concerned, though. That's my love for you. I hope that you know that I will do anything to have you back in my life. I'm only going to ask you this one last time. Anaya, can we please sit down and talk and work things out?"

"I really think that it would be best for both of us right now. You don't belong in Elmhurst, and I don't belong in this world of yours. We don't have too many options available right now. I'm also hurting, Kase; I really thought we had another shot at true happiness, but it was obviously not meant to be."

"But it can be, Anaya. You're letting the first little bump in the road derail our relationship. Seriously? After everything that we've been through over the years. You've never been able to form another relationship. I've already told you that the only reason I dated all these other women was to try and get you out of my head. And that failed horribly. Please, Anaya, I'm begging you!"

A total stubborn streak had set in with Anaya, and even though she knew she was being unreasonable with Kase, she couldn't lose face now.

Maybe she was right all along. Elmhurst was the right place for her. Or wasn't it? At this moment, she was so confused. She felt totally betrayed by Kase, and even though deep down she realized that maybe, just maybe, she had over-reacted, she couldn't turn back now.

"You know what, Anaya, on second thought; I'm not going to make you do anything that you are not totally comfortable with. If you want to go back to Elmhurst, then that's fine with me. I can't and won't force you to do anything ever again." Kase lost it completely.

"Hi, Mandy, Kase here! Please, could you arrange for a one-way ticket from Vegas to Arcata on the next flight? Uh-huh, the passenger's name is Anaya Mason... Thanks! Can you arrange for Mike or Jose, or whoever else is available, to drive her to the airport? Thanks."

"I've arranged for the concierge to book you a flight for this evening. She says that there's a flight leaving in the next hour and a half, giving you time to get to the airport. Anaya, are you really sure that this is how you want things between us to end?" She could hear the pain in his voice.

Their conversation was cut short by the phone ringing.

"Mr. Chapman, the car is ready to take Ms. Mason to the airport. Shall I send someone up to assist with the bags?"

"Yes, please!" Kase sounded totally exhausted as he put down the phone.

Kase could feel his heart racing again in his chest, which was not a good sign. He knew that he needed to calm down, or he was going to end up having to take more leave instead of trying to convince her to stay.

"I will always love you, no matter what happens. Thank you for bringing out the best in me. I'm not going to come downstairs with you. I wish you every happiness for the future, Anaya. I hope that someday you find exactly what you're looking for."

Opening the door for the bellhop, he hugged her on her way out. He could see that she'd been crying and was obviously also hurting through this whole misunderstanding. Watching her walk away from him for the second time was almost overwhelming for Kase to handle. Once he closed the door, he found the brandy and poured himself a double on the rocks.

Still, he was not entirely sure what to make of the situation. Something that had seemed so right had gone so terribly wrong, all in the space of a five-minute conversation with Vicky. Damn that woman. Could she seriously not have picked any other moment?

Anaya was heartbroken as she sat in the car to the airport. She sobbed her heart out all the way there. What has she done? Had she even made the right decision? Had she just blown her one chance at ever being truly happy? Her thoughts continued to haunt her all the way home.

CHAPTER 17
A Heart to Heart

KASE WAS FEELING MENTALLY, physically, and emotionally drained. He had even lost touch of what was happening at his hotels. Usually, he would wake up every morning, mentally and physically ready to take on the challenges of a brand new day. These last few days, however, he felt more inclined to want to pull the covers over his head and just stay there until someone from one of the casinos looked for him.

The natural passion and spark were missing from his routine work. Not even his meetings with the various casino managers and shareholders could get a reaction from him. Once again, it was Ethan Stone who picked up that there was something amiss with Kase. Pulling him aside in one of the passages, he asked Kase directly what was going on.

Kase knew better than to lie to Ethan, especially about anything medical. He explained everything to Ethan from the moment he left Vegas to go home, all about finding the love of his life again after all these years and how neither of them had really ever been able to move on. Kase gave Ethan the PG version of the story out of respect for Anaya. He told Ethan about his time in Elmhurst and how they grew closer together by working on community projects. Hell, he even talked about Joe Mason.

Looking to one of his oldest and most trusted friends for advice, Kase explained that almost everything in the hotel industry was beginning to lose its sparkle.

Kase had mentioned to Ethan years ago, when he was still a really young up-and-coming hotelier with only two casinos to his name, that whenever he started losing his passion, it might be time for him to consider packing it in. Kase knew that he had enough money and skills to offer his services as a contractor to hotels across the states, which could potentially resolve the Elmhurst/Vegas dilemma.

He kept hearing voices in his head, reminding him that when the passion and luster wear off, there's no coming back from that! What would it feel like to retire at thirty-two, though? It was definitely not something he'd actually planned for his career. Kase realized that he had his whole life in front of him—he could actually choose the path he wanted to follow.

From his very first day in the hotel industry, he had not stopped running. Initially, he worked at the bottom ranks of the ladder. Still, he had some exemplary mentors to teach him everything he put into practice today. These past few days, he has been feeling worse than he did before going home.

"Work has completely lost its appeal to me, Ethan, and I don't know what to do to get my mojo back again."

"What would you do if Anaya was here right now?" Kase sat up to take notice of that question because it was so straightforward and required a direct, no-nonsense answer.

"I would probably work harder than I've ever worked before because I need to prove myself to her and everyone else around me. I've even lost the will to go and socialize with any of the guys like we used to."

"I think you need to make another trip back home and see if you can patch things up with this girl, who sounds like the love of your life. If you can, great! If not, then you still have a lot of options, Kase. Don't give up just yet." Ethan had always been the wise one.

CHAPTER 18
Coming Home

FROM THE MOMENT Anaya boarded the airplane at Vegas airport, she knew she overreacted and made the wrong decision. She couldn't lose face, though, because that would prove to everyone that she was wrong. Anaya had such a competitive spirit that giving up was just not part of who she was. Why had she given up on Kase so quickly?

Having a lot of time to think on the flight back home, she realized that she'd let him slip through her fingers again. She knew that he was the one for her and that there would be no way that she'd be able to live without him, whether it was in Elmhurst or Vegas.

If she was being totally honest with herself, initially, the lifestyle freaked her out a little bit because she wasn't used to all the luxury. However, it was something she could definitely get on board with. She loved being pampered and fussed over, especially when it came from Kase. These were all small things that she noticed brought tremendous joy into his life.

Now that she had an idea of just three of his casino operations, she imagined how he managed to cope with another five. Her life was now a complete mess. Once she arrived back in Elmhurst, everywhere she looked seemed to remind her of Kase walking beside her. She knew deep down that he loved her. Why was she being so foolish in looking for ways to end it all with him? Why did she have to sabotage herself this way over and over again? This was exactly what she did with him the first time around. Was she actually afraid of long-term commitment?

She was invited to dinner with her mom and her dad. At dinner, she barely touched her food. Joe was really worried about his daughter and her sullen mood.

"We broke up." Anaya was hardly able to get the words out in between her sobs.

"What happened?" Diana was trying to get as much information out of her daughter as possible.

"He wants me to go and live there with him, but I don't know if I can give up the life I've built here in Elmhurst. This is the only home that I've ever really known." Anaya realized that this was precisely why she acted and reacted toward Kase as she did. She was afraid. Her main fear was change. She was too scared to venture out of her own personal little bubble that she'd created for herself here.

"Why don't you at least go and give it a try? You still have the rest of the summer holidays to make up your mind about whether you're happy about being there or whether you would rather be here. It doesn't sound like you gave poor Kase much of a chance." Once again, Diana had hit the nail right on the head. "My child, life is all about give and take and being able to make sacrifices for the ones you love. If it means taking some chances, you may have to be prepared to jump in with both feet first, but the decision to jump needs to be yours!"

"Thanks for all the advice, Mom. I really needed some straight-talking advice tonight. Thanks for dinner. Now I'm going to go home and do some research tonight!"

Opening her laptop, she began searching for teaching jobs in Vegas. Anaya couldn't believe the number of opportunities that were available and decided to send her application to several of them. Next, she looked for the first flight out of Arcata to Vegas. She didn't want to waste one more moment without being with the man she loved. If it meant she needed to take some risks, then that was what she was prepared to do. Finding a commercial flight, she booked it online. Now, it was time to pack. This time, she at least knew what she was in for. She double-checked her luggage allowance and weight restrictions, ensuring that each of her bags were fully compliant.

Anaya was so excited that she knew she was going to battle to get any sleep. Deciding to make herself a cup of tea to help her relax, she put the kettle on.

Startled by the sound of her doorbell, Anaya looked at the clock. It was 11:00 p.m. She wondered if there was an emergency of some sort, which made her heart skip a beat. She opened the door, and Kase was on her doorstep!

"I don't mind where I live. Without you, I have no home. I want to spend the rest of my life with you. If this is the town you want to stay in, then so be it."

She confessed she had a flight first thing in the morning to Vegas to find him. "I'm ready to be anywhere. I lost you once, and I don't want that to be the case ever again."

Anaya invited him into the house, and they shared a very tender embrace. Kase suddenly pulled away from her.

Going down on one knee, he held out a beautiful velvet box, opening it slowly.

"Anaya Mason, will you do me the honor of becoming Mrs. Kase Chapman?"

Anaya couldn't stop jumping up and down.

"Yes, yes, and one hundred times yes! You are the only man I ever want to be with. It may have taken me a while, but I will follow you to the ends of the earth, Kase!"

Only then did she look at the massive diamond ring that was set in a perfect setting to match her.

"This is just perfect, Kase. I love it, and I love you!"

"Please tell me that we can go back to Vegas. I honestly don't think that I gave it enough time to grow on me."

"Anaya, whatever you want, it's yours. It has always been yours since you were that crazy young kid in the seventh grade. I just think that I love you way more now than I ever thought it was possible to love another human being. The jet is ready to fly us back tomorrow if that's what you want."

"My bags are already packed!"

"One more thing, Miss Mason." Kase picked her up and carried her to her bed. "Can we please get some sleep? I have hardly slept since you left Vegas, and I'm exhausted."

"Sure, Kase. I'm so content right now, just being back in your arms. Promise me it will always be like this." Kase was fast asleep. Anaya couldn't believe that she was finally going to become Mrs. Kase Chapman. She couldn't believe that she'd landed the jackpot. It was all that she ever wanted.

A second chance romance is what you'll find when thrill-seeker Reece Hunter enters the Two Fox Bar wanting Cristina Fox after a one-night stand. If you want to learn their twists and turns, then take a peek at *The Billionaire and the Biker Chick*, Book 4 of the *Can't Buy a Billionaire Series*.

Grab your copy today!

Enjoy the preview!

Prologue

SHE WOKE up drenched in sweat, her hand searching all over the bed for him, but the only thing that met her touch was a cold, empty space. Her heart skipped a beat as she remembered that he was never coming back. He had chosen to give up on them, leaving her with nothing but heartache. She rolled over to his side of the bed and deeply inhaled his scent; it had slowly begun to fade over the six months since he left. There she lay, relishing in the pain as happiness had once again escaped her completely.

She wanted so desperately to move on. To find someone new, but she couldn't bring herself to do it. He had been the only man in her bed for three years, and her life felt so perfect during this time. But now nothing made sense to her. How could a person just walk away from something so significant without even thinking about it twice? She should've known this was how it would have ended. After all, he had been at the florist all the time, yet he never brought her flowers.

How could she have been stupid enough to believe he'd stay after all of the stories that circled about her and Zoe? She thought he knew her better than to believe their words over hers, and yet, when he came to say his goodbyes, it hit her harder than a train. The depression clawed at her soul, making her skin crawl with disgust at herself. She wanted out so bad. She needed to escape the dark cloud that hung over her head and shield herself from the bright light of the sun. Still, instead, she pushed herself deeper into the pillow, hoping to catch another whiff of his scent before it left her as well.

The sadness had become like a drug, an addiction she couldn't shake, not that she had the energy to even try and fight it. So instead, she buried herself deeper in the sheets, hoping, praying that he'd magically come to his senses and find his way back to her—to them. Deep down, she knew it was foolish to hope. It had happened already. Every person in her life had made a point to tell her too, but it was much easier to hope than accept the reality of the situation.

Even her mother had grown tired of her pity party. Every day, she would come over just after nine in the morning. While her mother was there, she would beg her daughter to get up because life was passing her by. She didn't care, instead allowing the sadness to consume her once more.

It wasn't until two months later that she got up and had breakfast like she did before the breakup, shortly after the eight-month mark. She showered, washed her hair, did her make-up, and put on her favorite clothes. She was done grieving a man who wasn't dead. In her den of depression, she decided then and there that it was time to start living again. Time to take back what was hers and fight for her own happiness. Even if it meant losing everything in the process.

She owed it to herself to live life to the fullest. On the other hand, she had no idea how to do it.

About the Author

Rose M. Cooper read her first novel when she was eight years old. Since then, she has read tens of novels and twice as many short stories. She, however, did not discover her special knack for writing romance fiction until a decade later.

Now a full-time author with a specialty in contemporary romance, Cooper writes sensual yet relatable love stories designed to hook her readers at first glance. She views writing as another outlet to creativity, and thus has no intentions of setting down her pen just yet. There are many intriguing love stories to be told, and Cooper is set to tell them all.

She hails from New York and currently makes her home in Copiague, New York with her husband, her black cat and her Maine Coon cat. When she is not writing, you will most certainly find her around computers or getting her nose stuck in a book.

facebook.com/RoseMaeCooper

twittcr.com/rosemaecooper

instagram.com/rosemaecooper

tiktok.com/@rosemaecooper

amazon.com/author/rosemaecooper

Support Me By Leaving A Review!

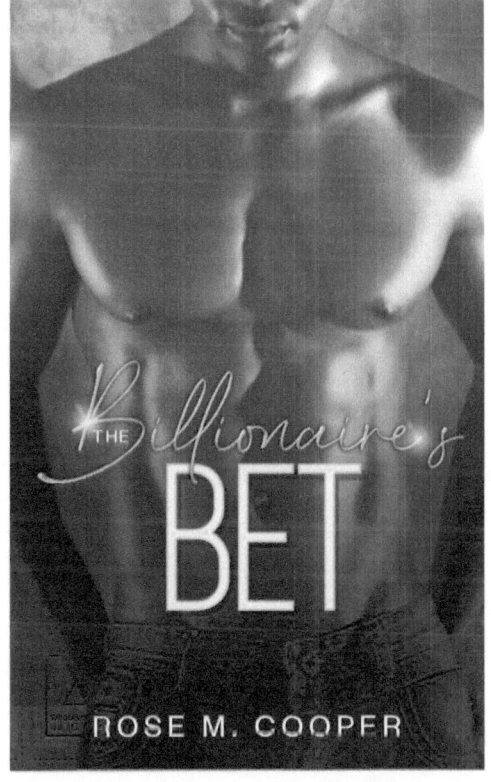

rosemaecooper.com/The_Billionaire's_Bet_book